ALL PASSION SPENT

ALL PASSION SPENT

Zaheda Hina

Translated from the Urdu by
Neelam Hussain

ZUBAAN

an imprint of Kali for Women
128 B Shahpur Jat, 1st floor
NEW DELHI 110 049
Email: zubaan@gmail.com and zubaanwbooks@vsnl.net
Website: www.zubaanbooks.com

First published by Zubaan 2011

Copyright © Zaheda Hina for the Urdu original, *Na Janoon Raha Na Pari Rahi*
Copyright © Neelam Hussain for the English translation
This edition published in 2017

10 9 8 7 6 5 4 3 2 1

ISBN 9789385932199 (HB)

Zubaan is an independent feminist publishing house based in New Delhi with a strong academic and general list. It was set up as an imprint of India's first feminist publishing house, Kali for Women, and carries forward Kali's tradition of publishing world quality books to high editorial and production standards. *Zubaan* means tongue, voice, language, speech in Hindustani. Zubaan is a non-profit publisher, working in the areas of the humanities, social sciences, as well as in fiction, general non-fiction, and books for children and young adults under its Young Zubaan imprint.

Typeset by RECTO graphics, New Delhi 110 096
Printed at Repro Knowledgecast Limited, Thane

For

my beloved grandchildren

Parma

and

Farjad

Birjees Dawar Ali stepped out of the lift onto the polished sheen of Italian marble. The air-conditioned hotel lobby hummed with the rise and fall of muted laughter and the susurration of many conversations as travellers came together, met and departed. The mirrored walls of the coffee shop enacted the lie of specious plenitude. From the many-branched chandelier waterfalls of light cascaded into old forgotten tunes picked out by the man at the piano.

Around her there was adornment and wealth; there was luxury, there was pleasure, and the illusion of pleasure. How different from the first, was this second meeting with the city. A new land and a new sky. The grim, dimly lit railway station. Hurrying coolies in patched, vari-coloured shirts burdened with luggage and on the platform a procession of vendors with trays and barrows and cries of 'Hot Tea'. The floors and walls spattered and stained with sprays of betel juice. Gobs of spittle abuzz with flies, and the crush of people, like a flood, in which she was tossed about like a straw, seeking familiar faces.

How different was this return. Every year a new year's card had made its way to her—intimation that light still shone in the windows of the house; and every year her card had travelled back, signifying life and presence. Then, a brief scrawl and bad news.

So many times she had been wrung with the longing to return. And every time, year after year she had stayed her heart. The heart protested: life is on the ebb. Shadows lengthen. How long will you delay?

And she? All these years she had lived in an alien time borrowed from others. *Doley naina mat khayo ... wanton eyes, tear-blurred ... how long could their message be denied*—how long could she go on deferring this moment of return? The face in the mirror mocked her and in her dreams, always, the open door, the light in the passage and then, the kindly faces.

The mirror upbraided her—

So afraid?

So faint hearted?

You were not so weak when you first travelled to this city?

But don't you see?

That was another time and another place.

Disinterested and without fear; her heart in one hand, her life on the other, she had undertaken her quest for the beloved—*youn kuay sanam main waqte safar, nazara baame naz kiya*—haunting the streets for a glimpse

The face in the mirror blurred.

It wasn't easy to gather the scattered shards of her heart. She was still trying to piece them together when the invitation from the United States arrived and another road opened up before her.

More barbs from the mirror: have you forgotten that you have eaten the salt of that house?

She is overcome. Salt? My very life is forfeit to that house.

Then admit it—you have betrayed your trust. When you heard the news; when that letter arrived—they must have waited for you.

The mirror would not be gainsaid.

It was true; she had failed to pay her dues. She bowed her head. Then let me come face to face with my life's truth. Let me go to them now, even if it is for a few days.

From Indira Gandhi International Airport to Jinnah terminal. Tension. Nervousness. I haven't informed them of my arrival. Should I just turn up? Unannounced? Blood drips from each sealed mouth. No. I'll leave my luggage at a hotel—a little time to collect myself, before I go to them.

The city had grown like a cancer. From the airport terminal to the hotel, leprous walls proclaimed messages of hate.

'AVENGE THE MARTYRDOM OF BABRI MASJID!'

'CRUSH INDIA!

'LONG LIVE SINDHI NATIONALISM!'

'SHIA INFIDELS!'

'DEATH FOR TREACHERY TO THE QUAID!'

'DEATH TO ALL QADIANIS!'

'WE'LL KILL AND BE KILLED FOR THE MUHAJIR PROVINCE!'

Here too the same slogans of hate pursued her. She shut her eyes. Her heart was beating fast when at last the taxi drove into the portico of the Marriott across the road from Frere Hall. The hotel was new, but the road to it was well traversed.

She stopped before one of the mirrors in the lobby and came face to face with a woman. A stately figure enfolded in a starched sari; shoulder length hair, with a touch of frost at the temples. Caught in the waterfall of light from the chandelier, the brooch on her sari opened its eyes and smiled.

Outside the hotel entrance, a rain laden evening and the city's hum. From the gnarled and ancient trees that lined the road the chirping of birds rose and fell in a whirlpool of noise.

She walked on slowly—Frere Hall, the American Consulate, Sindh Club, and State Guest House—on either side of the road familiar buildings came into view and receded till she reached the square outside the Metropole Residential Hotel. Across the road, a KLM model plane reared its head against a block of flats flats. She crossed over and walked to the main entrance. The wide steps of a banistered staircase led the way up. Slowly, reluctantly, she began to climb. The first floor was passed, then the second till finally the third was reached and she stood facing the double panelled wooden door. The old brass nameplate was tarnished. It was long since it had known the touch of polish and elbow grease. The walls breathed neglect and desertion. Overcome, she put out her hand to the wall for support. The doorbell was pressed and somewhere in the depths of the house she heard its muted ring. How unlike it was to the sharp imperative call of earlier times.

She stood there staring at the shut door, but it did not open. No sound of advancing footsteps fell on her ears. She pressed the bell again and then impatiently, for the third time. This time there was a faint answering call and the slow shuffle of advancing feet. Slowly, hesitantly, the door opened. The frail, bent figure of a woman stood at the threshold. A handful of bones in a brown cardigan and sari. The pallu was draped, Parsi style, on the right shoulder and a black skullcap hid the white hair. Propped up by a walking stick, the old crone craned her neck upwards and looked at Birjees.

Birjees looked past her. She could see no sign of Bano Aunty. Manuchehr must have employed this woman to keep his mother company.

'Is Mrs. Cowasjee in?' she asked.

Arthritic fingers held on to the door. 'Speak! What do you want?'

'I would like to see Mrs. Cowasjee,' Birjees' voice was a shade louder this time.

'Speak, baba, speak. I am Mrs. Cowasjee.'

'I am Mrs. Cowasjee!' 'I am Mrs. Cowasjee'. The echoes travelled up from the earth and echoed back from the sky. The voice fell on deaf ears, and she failed to recognize it. With blind eyes she looked at the woman standing before her. Tears, not blood coursed through her veins.

'I don't know you.' The tone was dismissive as the woman made to shut the door.

Birjees reached out and gripped the open door, 'I'm Birjees, Bano Aunty. *Your* Birjees. I've come from India.'

'India? Hindustan?' the voice strove for recognition. Suddenly lamps lit up beneath the dull faded skin. 'You have come Birjees? You have brought Meenu with you?' Trembling hands clasped her with what strength they could muster. Her hands found Bano aunty's crippled fingers and she clung to her in an embrace.

Time's squirrel-bright eyes fell upon Birjees Dawar Ali and Bano Lashkari Cowasjee as it nibbled away at the passing minutes.

❁ ❁ ❁

The rain fell steadily. There was a power failure; the dark heightened the night's desolation and filled the shadows with hidden menace. Sitting on the steps of the banistered staircase Birjees shuddered. The rain-laded monsoon air seeped into her clothes. She shivered in the chill damp air.

The advancing clip clop of a horse arose above the soughing of the wind and rain. Hooves slipped, stumbled and steadied again on the wet tarmac. A little distance above the ground a glow-worm light dipped, arose and drew steadily nearer. A flash of lightning lit up the night. Shrouded in canvas against the rain, a Victoria had stopped in front of the building. It caught the coachman in the act of alighting. Then the night surged in again and the glow-worm light of the Victoria's lantern was visible once more.

A match was struck inside the Victoria, and a scene reminiscent of an English movie flickered into motion. It occurred to her that the passengers were probably residents in the building and they would soon be upon her. The knot in her stomach tightened. What will these people think when they see me here? Will they not take me for a thief, a beggar—or worse—she was unable to complete the sentence, to give a name to her thoughts.

People had alighted from the Victoria and were heading swiftly towards the building. The match was struck to light the way and its tiny glow revealed the figures of a man and woman. Quickly, she stood up to let them pass. Startled the woman looked at her and said something under her breath, drawing her sari close to her as she went by. Her pallu was draped on the right shoulder. Perhaps she was a Parsi—there had been many Parsis in Calcutta and Bombay. The man flicked away the burnt match-end and followed the woman up the stairs.

She turned to look at the retreating figures. They were soon lost in the darkness and the shadows gathered around her once more. She put her head on her knees. Her temples throbbed with pain. What was she to do? Where was she to go? Was she to spend the whole night on these stairs? Fear coursed through her bones. She had never been so afraid in her life.

Perhaps it would be better to move higher up on the staircase instead of sitting on lowest step. At least she would be hidden from the night watchman and the eyes of every stray passer-by.

She moved up a few steps and had just sat down when something pricked her hand She felt around in the dark and her fingers encountered a small object. She picked it up. It was a brooch. Perhaps it belonged to the woman who had just gone up. Perhaps even now the couple was thinking of coming down to look for it. But when, after about ten minutes or so, nobody came she became fretful, irritated. Did she not have troubles enough without the added complication of the brooch? What was she to do about it? She couldn't just leave it to lie around on the stairs. She got up, clasping the leather strap of the bag that hung on her shoulder. To attempt to look for the apartment of two total strangers in pitch darkness would be another new experience.

Supporting herself against the wall on one side she cautiously made her way up the stairs. There was no point in knocking at the door on the first floor—the sounds of the couple's footsteps had gone further up.

Clutching the brooch in one hand, Birjees climbed on. By the time she reached the second floor, her hands were clammy and her heart was beating fast. Perhaps one of these two doors belonged to their flat? She knocked at the door on the left. A dim light shone through a crack. At her second knock a man's sharp voice asked in English, 'Who's there?'

She didn't know how to respond. She had never been in such a position before. 'Please open the door,' she replied, also in English.

After a few moments the door half opened and a face peered out. It was a Goanese face. The light from a kerosene lamp in the corridor behind him fell on the landing.

'What do you want at this time? Who are you looking for?' The voice was unsympathetic.

'The Parsi family who live in this building … '

'You want Cowasjee's flat?' he interrupted. 'Third floor; the door on the left.' The door slammed shut in her face.

Breathing a sigh of relief she resumed her climb. Perhaps this encounter with the Parsi family would help to solve her problem as well. She paused when she reached the third floor landing. The phosphorescent button of the call bell shone in the dark. She reached out her hand to press it, then drew it back and knocked instead. On the other side of the door, she could hear the voices of a man and a woman raised in speech. At the sound of the knock, she heard the woman say something in Gujarati. Quick footsteps came towards her and the door opened. A branched candlestand stood in the corridor lighting the figure of a man.

'Who are you? What do you want?' he asked as his sharp eyes examined her.

She looked straight at him, 'Has your wife lost something?' She was quite sure this was the man who had passed her by on the stairs not too long ago.

From inside a woman's voice arose questioningly.

'No, it is not Manuchehr. It's the girl from the stairs,' he replied.

She realized that probably they had been talking about her, wondering what she was doing on the stairs of their building so late at night. Perhaps this was Cowasjee.

'Yes, my wife dropped her brooch somewhere. Have you found it?'

She extended her arm and opened her hand. In the glow of the candlelight, a turquoise brooch gleamed on her sweaty palm. It looked valuable.

At that moment the woman stepped into the corridor.

'Come inside.' The man's tone was authoritative.

She hesitated, but the fear of a night on the stairs of a strange building overcame the fear of entering a strange flat. The man stood aside to let her pass and she stepped into a passage.

The woman looked at her suspiciously then turned questioningly towards the man, but he said nothing, merely gestured to Birjees to enter the room as he and the woman followed her in. She found herself in an elegant drawing room. A double branched light showed her a rich carpet, sofas upholstered in velvet, small tables and walls covered with framed portraits and landscapes.

The man gestured towards the sofa, inviting her to sit. Puzzled, the woman stared at her.

'This girl has brought you your brooch,' he said addressing his wife; then turned towards Birjees: 'give the brooch to her.'

She got up and extended the brooch towards the woman whose eyes had opened in surprise. She looked at Birjees, 'Good girl! Where did you find it?' she asked turning the brooch around in her fingers.

'On the stairs. You must have dropped it there.'

'What made you think it belonged to us?'

'Parsi women normally wear brooches on their saris.'

'But how did you find our flat?' He interrogated her like a legal prosecutor.

'I tried the second floor flat. I was told that you lived on the third floor.'

'You could have kept the brooch for yourself.' The implication sent the blood rushing to her face.

'I do not keep what does not belong to me,'

'I'm sorry; I did not mean to cast doubts on your honesty. It's just that the way you were sitting on the steps downstairs …' he stopped, leaving the sentence unfinished. Perhaps he was unable to find the words that would express his thoughts without giving offence.

'I was taken aback when I saw you sitting there. I said to Cowasjee, I said, there is something suspicious going on here. Now don't mind me, but our intentions are not written on our foreheads for all to see.' Mrs. Cowasjee spoke fast, rushing to the end of the sentence.

'I thought I had dropped the brooch in the Victoria— that it could've fallen on the stairs didn't even enter my

mind—It's a family heirloom. It was my grandmother's.'
She was silent for a few minutes. 'I don't know how to
thank you for bringing it back to me.'

The light bulbs gave a tentative flicker before the room
sprang to life. The power had been restored.

'Thanks be to Ahura Mazda!'

Mr. and Mrs. Cowasjee's eyes examined Birjees from
head to toe, travelling from the strained and tense though
not unattractive face, the clean but simple cotton clothes,
the pair of feet in Kohlapuri chapals, to the modest leather
bag that lay on the floor beside them.

She longed to ask them to let her stay, to grant her
sanctuary for the night. She picked up her bag and stood
up to take her leave.

'Just a minute.' Cowasjee cleared his throat. 'I assume
you were on your way home when the downpour caught
you,' he said, looking straight into her eyes. 'Our son will
be home soon. Stay till he comes and we will drive you
home.'

'Yes,' speech dwindled into silence; with an effort she
picked up the narrative thread: 'this is my first day in
Karachi. I arrived today, and I haven't been able to locate
the relatives, with whom I am to stay,' she faltered, unable
to find the words that would take her sentence to its logical
conclusion.

'Good God! You mean you couldn't find your relations
and were planning to spend the night on the stairs? Is that
why you were sitting there?' Disbelief and amazement vied

for place in Cowasjee's voice. 'Which fool told you that you could just walk into a city like Karachi in this way? Did you not inform your relatives of your arrival?

Birjees bowed her head. What was there for her say? How could she unfold the tale of her woes to a stranger?

Mrs. Cowasjee looked at her with perceptive eyes. 'My poor child, was there no one at home to accompany you?'

Giving her no time to reply, Cowasjee interrupted: 'Your name?'

'Birjees.'

'Where are you from?'

Before she could answer, the shrill tones of the door bell intervened, disrupting the interrogation.

'That must be Manuchehr,' muttered Cowasjee getting up.

'He's very late today,' Mrs. Cowasjee interjected softly.

'When is he not late? He's really inconvenienced us tonight by taking the car,' he grumbled moving towards the door.

A moment later she heard the door open followed by a sharp, quick exchange in Gujarati. Footsteps came down the passage and were lost in some other room. Cowasjee returned to the drawing room: 'I'm sure you haven't eaten all day.'

Head slightly bowed, her eyes silently traced the pattern on the carpet.

'I haven't eaten yet either. Stay here while I heat up some food.' Mrs. Cowasjee got up purposefully.

'I'll talk to you later. We're just going to have dinner, why don't you go and freshen up before we eat.' Cowasjee showed her the way to the bathroom.

A spotless washbasin and bathtub sparkled in the bright electric light. Their milky whiteness hurt the eyes. Shampoo, cologne, after-shave and other toiletries were arrayed neatly in the cabinet. Birjees looked at herself in the mirror. Is this really I? Without a name and with nowhere to go? She felt a sudden rush of tears. Bending over the washbasin she turned on the tap. The water gushed out and she tucked up her sleeves to wash away the grime and dust from her face and arms, then passed wet hands over her hair and tried to give it a semblance of order before stepping out.

The dining room bore witness to generations of comfortable living. She cast a cursory glance around the room before sitting down on the chair indicated by Mrs. Cowasjee. The table had been laid only for three. Mrs. Cowasjee passed each dish to her but the experience of eating at a strange table was so alien, so novel, that the food seemed to stick in her throat and despite her hunger, she found it difficult to swallow more than a few morsels. During the meal, Mrs. Cowasjee maintained a flow of inconsequential small talk, but Cowasjee ate in complete silence and did not utter a word.

The meal over, she hesitantly asked to help clear the table and the offer was accepted with alacrity. This household chore dispensed with, Mrs. Cowasjee took her back to the drawing room, said something rapidly in Gujarati to Cowasjee and went out again. Cowasjee followed her.

Perhaps they wanted to consult with each other about what next to do with her.

In times long past a huge flood of humanity had moved from one place to another. There were the good and the bad among the exchange of populations that took place. The wounded and the dispossessed, as well as those who fooled the world with masquerades of loss and injury. Sunk deep in thought, Birjees struggled with her own dilemma. It was not so long ago, after all, when the wall of the high citadel had been breached and its inhabitants had seen their world destroyed. When the princesses—Gul Bano, Mehr Bano, Khurshid Jamal, Meh Jamal—had washed dishes and served in the homes of the Mewati and Jat castes, gone a begging in the streets, had sought shelter in shrines and graveyards; found sanctuary in brothels.

Laden with a pair of milk white pillows and brightly coloured bed sheets, Cowasjee re-entered the room with quick determined steps and unburdened his load on the sofa.

'You may sleep on one of the sofas tonight. If there is anything else that you need, please don't hesitate to ask, but I would have you know that I'm a lawyer, and every day I come across all kinds of people in my professional life. If you have committed any crime and are evading pursuit, you will not be able to get away with it; nor will you be able to deceive me for long.' He paused, took a deep breath and looked searchingly at her. 'You appear to be from a good family, and girls from such homes don't come without bag and baggage, searching their relations in strange cities.

If this is an attempt at a runaway marriage, then let me remind you, that families have a way of implicating those who innocently and in good faith, offer help to such girls.'

He waited for an answer and Birjees, helpless in the face of his disbelief, could think of nothing to say.

'There are times when a person's silence can be taken as evidence of guilt. Anyhow, here are your pillows and bed sheets. Bolt the door after me. I will talk to you tomorrow morning.' He left the room without looking at her and shut the door behind him.

Birjees had not expected this stern treatment from Cowasjee. Perhaps if he had not been a lawyer, his manner would have been different. She got up, bolted the door and collapsed on the divan.

No sooner had she eased her limbs on this temporary, makeshift bed that her own bed and her own room came to mind. She recalled the past, the people whom she had loved so dearly and who had loved her. They were lost to her now. The very dust that owned her, the earth that had nourished her and made what she was; where had it all gone? Had it been wise to leave it all? To give up everything for this new land? Had she after all, failed to make the right decision?

Tormented by these thoughts she changed her drift to Cowasjee and how, in his authoritarian way, he had made it amply clear that she would have to disclose her full story to him the following day. But what was there that she could tell him about herself? She had kept nothing away that was worth hiding. She had told him the truth and he had refused to believe her. Overwhelmed by her own helplessness, she hid her face in the pillow; it smelt faintly of potpourri. By coming here, she had forfeited all such fragrances, left them all behind her.

❂ ❂ ❂

The smell of freshly brewed coffee soothed Naushervan Pervaiz Cowasjee's nerves. Spent between waking and sleeping, his night had been restless, and he had finally got up to work on his book.

There had been no exchange of confidences about the girl between him and his wife that night, yet he knew that her wound, still green, had opened and bled. The small choking sounds from the figure by his side had not escaped him, yet he had done nothing, spoken no word of comfort to her.

Protected by her ignorance, Bano could weep. He had no such recourse and the very knowledge, that was denied his wife, closed all avenues of comfort to him. He had spent that night on the ninety-seventh threshold of Dastoor Shahzada's kingdom· face to face with the Truth therein:

'When any one departs to the other world it is not proper for others that they should utter an outcry, maintain grief, and make lamentation and weeping. Because every tear that issues from the eyes becomes a drop of that river that flows

before the bridge of Chinwat, and the soul of that dead
person remains at that place, … and it is not possible to pass
over the Chinwat bridge.' (Avesta: Yasna: 49: 10)

He knew that the river that flowed between his loved
ones and safety was made up of his tears. That these tears,
in which they floundered as they strove to bridge the
unsurpassable distance between them and Pul-e-Chinwat,
would not let them see that the bridge, with its illusion of
safety, was razor sharp and fine as the blade of a sword.

Picking up the mug of coffee, he left the kitchen. Pausing
briefly outside the door of the drawing room where the
girl lay sleeping, he went into his study and switched
on the light. The room sprang to life. Placing the coffee
mug on the table he turned and looked at the portrait of
Zarathustra that hung on the wall. The haloed figure of
the prophet with his bull-headed staff and white and gold
robes stood against a blue translucent sky that merged with
the pink and orange line of the horizon held his gaze for a
moment. He had bought it in Bombay, from Pithawalla.
The number of houses where this picture could be found
had dwindled. They were fast disappearing reminders of
an almost extinct people and their increasingly extinct life
style.

Lifestyles, rituals, the small routine observances that give
one a sense of home in the world are the most vulnerable
to time's erasures and are always the first to go. This
girl—whose face and bearing bore witness to breeding and
social status—what were the circumstances that had led

her to their door, a supplicant for a night's shelter? Such things had never happened before. Life that had flowed like a placid river, unchanged and unchanging, was now a whirlpool of muddied waters, uncertain, unpredictable.

The wheel of time had scattered families, crushing and displacing peoples as it hurtled along, spreading havoc in its wake. The stroke of a pen divided countries, sharing out the severed pieces among contending parties and men hunted men like beasts of prey transforming homesteads and communities into towers of silence watched over by vultures

It was not too long ago when he too had been faithful to each observance, steadfast and constant at every step. But all that belonged to the past, to the time before all boundaries were transgressed and all the stages of gain and loss, of pain and renunciation traversed. It had taken him a long time to accept that change and time's evanescence were the only constants—indifferent, without limits, infinite.

He picked up Mullah Mohsin Fani's book. His roots lay deep in the Zoroastrian faith. Its teachings were his articles of belief. He understood that one revolution of Saturn was the equivalent of one day, that thirty such days made a month and twelve months marked the limits of one year and ten lakh years added up to one unit of time; that the sum of ten lakh planetary rotations was equal to a 'fard'; that ten lakh fards added up to one 'vard' and ten lakh vard were equal to one 'mard'. Ten lakh mard in turn made one 'jad' and three thousand jad made a 'vad' and two thousand vad were the equal on one 'zad'.

He was familiar with the text; had read it many times, and every time the same question had accosted him: what lay beyond 'zad'. Did zad mark the beginning of infinity? The Infinite—*Az toomi pursum, az toomi pursum ... This I ask Thee, O Ahura, tell me truly who by procreation is the primal father of Truth? Who created the course of the sun and stars? Through whom does the moon wax and wane? These very things and others I wish to know, O Mazda.* (Avesta: Yasna: 44)

Questions! So many questions! But no answers—only silence and the onward rush of relentless time. He had never believed in the image of Time as a benign old man with a shining visage and flowing beard. The high priests of ancient Persia had taught him to imagine it differently, as a glowing youth, refulgent, strong, beautiful, clear-sighted. But time was neither an old man nor a beautiful boy—blind, mute and deaf it hurtled along grinding to dust and destroying all that strayed in its path

Many, many years ago in Paris, he had seen the Parsi scholar, Agha Pur Daud, shed tears over the fate of their princesses humiliated and sold in the marketplace and streets of Madina after the Arab onslaught. Castigating the desecrations of time, he had wept for the thinkers and poets compelled to sacrifice their integrity and honour at the altar of the conquering power and depict their race as an effete and tired people whose time was past. At that time he had been busy with the translation of the *Gathas* from Persian into English and his home had been the meeting place of Parsi students from England and India. Although a Muslim by birth, his pride lay in his Persian and Aryan roots. It was from him that the young Gujarati speaking Naushervan Pervez Cowasjee who, despite owning to the Parsi belief system had known little of his own history, had discovered the ancient lore of the Zoroastrians, and lost his heart to his Persian heritage.

They had talked at length of the vagaries and vicissitudes of time, and their discussions had deepened his understanding of the unpredictable complexity of history, but Agha Pur Daud had failed to fathom its mysteries and to understand that time could not be limited to one dimension alone, that like the sacred flame, it had many aspects, many guises. In one of its guises, it takes pause, to provide room for the leisurely shaping of individual lives and cultures—in another guise, it rushes inexorably on, indifferent to the fate of nations and peoples, trampling all that lies in its path. Who could have guessed that one day in the unforeseen future, there would come a night when Cowasjee's house would provide shelter to a young co-religionist of Agha Pur Daud?

He sipped his coffee and his thoughts went back to his college days when he had acted as Julius Caesar in a college play. He remembered when after the 'et tu brute' line, he had clutched at his breast and fallen; the little sac of red dye had resisted the secret pressure of his hand and failed to burst. Unnerved, he had made a hash of the scene and the college hall had rung with laughter. It was Ghulam Hussain Sindhi as Anthony who had made the speech over Caesar's prostrate body and helped him off the stage. Sindhi had risen to become a well-known actor, but that was the last time that Cowasjee was part of that antic world.

He had not known then that time was the biggest illusionist of all; that when he clutched his breast to fall on life's stage, there would be no Ghulam Hussain Sindhi at hand to help him rise. That he would have to struggle to his feet himself; that he would stand up and walk, go to court, argue his cases, immerse himself in life's routine, and continue to live.

Somewhere in the house a door opened and the sound of footsteps cut across his thoughts. He felt as if he was waking from a dream. These weren't Bano's footsteps. It must be the girl. Last night she had told him that her name was Birjees. Birjees—the planet Mercury, which is also called auspicious; the celestial arbiter that shines bright in the sixth of the seven firmaments. He took a deep breath and closed Mullah Mohsin Fani's book.

Birjees opened her eyes to the window curtains flapping in the breeze. For a few moments she couldn't remember where she was, then memory asserted itself and she sat up in agitation. It was almost daylight and soon she would have to face Cowasjee's questions. She lay back, uncertain about what to do. It was a little past dawn and the household still slept. A deep silence pervaded the house. In a little while they would awaken.

It had never been easy for her to reveal her innermost thoughts even to those who were close to her, but to have to do so to complete strangers was more than she could bear. She got up, folded the sheets, shook out the pillows and patted them into shape then made her way to the bathroom. Her ablutions done, she tip-toed back to the drawing room; she wanted to leave the house as quickly as possible. Force of circumstance had compelled her to seek shelter here for the night, but that did not mean that she should unfold her tale of woe to its inmates.

Taking out her pen she tore a page from her diary and wrote a brief note of thanks and placed it on the centre table. Casting a fleeting glance around the room, she slung her bag on her shoulder and stepped out. The clock on the adjacent wall showed her that it was six thirty in the morning. Walking softly down the corridor she reached the main door. It opened with a faint click. Paralysed, she stood there for a moment, then stepped out softly and shut the door, gently releasing the handle of the automatic lock. Now the door could not be opened from the outside.

She drew a deep breath. This house had given her shelter at a time of extreme crisis in her life, and here she was, escaping from it like a guilty thing as if its inmates had visited some nameless tyranny on her. For a moment doubt stirred in her mind. Was she doing the right thing in leaving like this? Or was this too, like her arrival in this city, a hasty and ill-considered act? Perhaps she should have stayed and solicited the lawyer's help in tracing Pervaiz and his family. Perhaps—but the threshold had been crossed and it was no longer possible to retrace her steps. Wrestling with her thoughts, trying to hold back the sudden rush of tears, she began her descent of the wooden stairs.

Suddenly the landing filled with light and Cowasjee's imperative tones echoed down the stairwell:

'Wait, Birjees!'

Like a bolt of lightning, his voice fell on her and she swung round to face it. Time slowed down and took on a dreamlike quality. Hope, relief, longing vied with each other for ascendancy. The light streamed out from the open door and was lost along the stairs. Cowasjee was standing in the doorway. Silhouetted against the light his figure was giant-like. Mingled disbelief and outrage had given an edge to his command. It fell like a whiplash on her body raising weals that throbbed and burned with shame.

Her feet slipped and faltered in the slime of humiliation and she prayed that all this was a bad dream from which she would awaken, knowing all the while that the wish was futile. Trying to look defeat in the face she raised her head and retraced her steps.

Cowasjee moved away from the door and Birjees crossed the passage and entered the drawing room. It was a puppet show. The master puppeteer pulled one set of strings and Cowasjee moved back. Then he twitched the next set of strings and she moved forward with small jerking steps.

Weighing her on the scales of truth and reliability, Cowasjee seemed unable to arrive at any clear conclusion. 'Perhaps it is a habit with you to go through life making hasty and ill-considered decisions?' He frowned, 'I have no time for such stupid behaviour!'

She had expected him to deal harshly with her; that he would scold her, in the way Abba Mian had been used to do, was something she had not even come near to imagining.

Through lowered lids she examined the peacocks, parrots, deer and cheetahs on the carpet. It reminded her of the carpet in Abba Mian's room. With its many coloured birds, beasts, trees and flowers intertwined with characters from Omar Khayyam against a cream background. It had been very like the one in this room.

'We gave you shelter for the night; no one dragged you here by force. What then was the need to slip away like this?'

'I ... you ... I did not want to burden you further...' she faltered. 'I left a note for you, explaining ...' Like thorns, the words stuck in her throat.

"Quiet! Not one word more of your puerile philosophy,' he stormed. Then mimicked her tones: 'I did not want to be a burden! My foot! And where, may I ask, is that momentous note?' Then his eyes fell on the scrap of paper under the ashtray and picking it up, he glanced through it. 'What poor judges of people you young folk are and what impossible situations you land yourselves in. Just because the night had passed, you thought you had become an unbearable burden for us? Thank your lucky stars that I was awake. What guarantee did you have that alone, in a strange city, you would once again find a home as safe as this one?'

Head bent, Birjees sat there speechless. Had he called her self-centred, accused her of ingratitude, she would have found it possible to face him, but he was scolding her—like Abba Mian.

'But enough of that! Now sit up straight and tell me about yourself.'

She opened her bag and took out a large manila envelope. Opening it she took out her passport and Master's Degree and handed them to him. He looked at the Masters Degree and then at her; then back again at the piece of paper in his hand. Returning it to her, he began to leaf through her passport.

'And you thought this journey too was like commuting between Calcutta and Patna? To be undertaken whenever the fancy took you? Don't you realise that this is a matter of two countries; a question of international borders and boundaries?' His voice was tinged with impatience. 'What I fail to understand is how your family allowed you to undertake this journey on your own?' He paused, took off his spectacles and cleaned the lens on the silk sleeve of his dressing gown.

Mrs. Cowasjee peeped in at the door. Greeting them both, she turned to her husband: 'O, Baba! So early in the morning you have begun to badger and beat at the girl's brains. She needs to eat her breakfast, not her brains, at this time. You advocate folk are very difficult I must say.' She came and sat down next to Birjees. 'My dear, don't you worry. Day and night my husband does this question-answer in court, and now he can't stop. It has become a habit with him and all the time he does it.'

Hiding a smile at her individual style, she wondered what Mrs. Cowasjee would think if she knew that she had tried to sneak away from her house early that morning.

'I'm going to get breakfast ready, so the two of you get ready too,' and she left the room.

On further questioning by Cowasjee, Birjees told him that she had informed her relatives about her arrival but there had been no one to meet her at the station. Then when she finally made her way to their house, it was to discover that they had moved to another place. It was possible that they had never received her letter and telegram. She had made enquiries among the neighbours but they had left no forwarding address. She herself had no idea about the whereabouts of other family members living in this city.

The interrogation was still continuing when Mrs. Cowasjee walked in and stood before them, arms akimbo.

'O, Baba, I'm telling you! Is this court scene ending or not ending? Have mercy on the girl, Baba! Go! Shave and take a shower and let her take a shower too. Manuchehr will be waking up soon and then he'll start beating his kettledrum.'

She took Birjees by the arm. 'I've forgotten your name. Very short, my memory.'

Turning to look at Cowasjee, she saw him slip her passport into the pocket of his dressing gown.

'Don't worry, I'm not going to run away with it,' he said, aware of the unspoken question in her eyes.

She followed Mrs. Cowasjee into the lounge. A huge Grundig radiogram stood against one wall. Boxes of His Master's Voice records hid the surface of an adjacent table. A harmonium lay on the takht against the further wall. She was overcome by an intense longing for home.

'Do you want to iron your clothes?'

'Yes please. They're all squashed and crumpled up in my bag.'

'I'll get the iron and the ironing board.'

Mrs. Cowasjee left the room and Birjees took out a suit of clothes from her bag. Yesterday evening she had stuffed two suits along with her papers and jewellery in her overnight bag. Her two suitcases she had left at the house in P.I.B Colony that only a few weeks ago, had been home to Ashraf Chacha and his family. It was her good luck that the old matriarch who seemed to rule the house now, had succumbed to a kind impulse. Otherwise she would have had to lug her suitcases all over the city.

Mrs. Cowasjee returned, dragging the ironing board with her. 'Quick! Quick! Do your ironing. This morning time goes in a blink of the eye. Breakfast will be ready as soon as you and that advocate of mine have showered. Soon Manuchehr will awaken and start kicking up a fuss: '"where are my shoes?" "Where is my tie?" Array, baba, you came home at midnight, you changed in your room, so that's where all your things will be. Exactly where you are! Then, when he's dressed, it will be, "why is my omelette cold?" "Why is my toast dry?" Will somebody tell him,

"Mister, when you sleep till midday, then how will your omelette be hot?'"

The uninterrupted flow of words followed her as she left the room and Birjees, having ironed her clothes made her way to the bathroom. Washing away the grime and dirt of the journey under the shower, enveloped in the scent of soap that seemed to enter her very pores, she felt she was in her own home. The tiredness of the long journey, the searching eyes that had failed to find the expected faces at the station, the despair and vexation, the salt of tears shed in the night, were washed away in the stream of water that flowed off her body leaving her cleansed and refreshed.

Standing in front of the mirror, she dried her hair as her thoughts turned to Cowasjee. How like Chacha Roshan Rai he was in speech and mien. He had been another one to split hairs. But he did not scold. While this gentleman scolded and harangued exactly like Abba Mian. She stood in front of the mirror struggling with the tangles in her hair. That job done, she left the bathroom and made her way to the kitchen. Mrs. Cowasjee turned to look at her and went on staring. 'Now you look like a human being. You're very beautiful Birjees.' Embarrassed by the unexpected spontaneity of the remark she looked at her, then realised that Mrs. Cowasjee's eyes had filled with sudden tears.

'I must have got a green chilli seed in my eye,' she said, turning aside to look for something in the china cupboard. Birjees looked at her in amazement. There wasn't a green chilli in sight, then how had its seed got in her eye?

The two of them entered the dining room with the tea tray and the rest of the breakfast paraphernalia to find a bathed and shaved Cowasjee in spotless white, his spectacles on his nose, immersed in the morning paper. His silver grey hair stirred faintly under the ceiling fan and the toaster hummed contentedly. Two slices of toast popped up just as she sat down, and the humming ceased. Mrs. Cowasjee stuck two more slices of toast in the toaster and began to butter the ones that had been done.

Even at this meal, there was no sign of Manuchehr. Perhaps he normally kept late hours and slept late in the mornings. Mrs. Cowasjee handed her a piece of buttered toast and put the other on her husband's plate. Cowasjee was peeling a boiled egg and at the same time trying to prevent the pages of the newspaper from flapping in the breeze stirred up by the fan. The entire scene presented a picture of safe, stable, deeply rooted domesticity.

Abba Mian raises his eyes from the *The Times of India*, folds it and places it on the side. A bowl of porridge lies before him, there are boiled eggs in the eggcups. Large white china plates with a blue line hold fried eggs like sunflowers. The room is redolent with the scent of homemade guava jelly. There is a wedge of cheese in front of her. She cuts off tiny pieces and pops them in her mouth.

'I'm not going to eat anything.' Bhai is demanding a kachauri and potato bhaji breakfast, and Abba Mian, scraping the burnt bits of toast with a knife, is lending him his full support. Chhotti Ammi glares at him for spoiling Bhaiya.

Ruqaiya bua and Kaneezan bua bustle in and out of the room bringing fresh tea in a pot and hot kachauris.

Nudrat puts a spoonful of egg yolk in her mouth and says, 'Apajani, quickly tell me the answer to my riddle: "one is yellow the other is blue. The one who finds the true answer lives. Out of the live one comes the dead one and out of the dead one comes the live one."' Before she can answer, Nudrat begins to chant, 'you can't guess! You can't guess! Apajani's lost! Apajani's lost! Apajani, the correct answer is egg.' She goes off into a peal of triumphant laughter and continues to chuckle long after the joke is over. Chhotti Ammi looks at her through narrowed eyes and the sharp disapproval wipes the laughter from her face.

Mrs. Cowasjee pushed a cup of hot tea towards her and the image dissolved in the steam and was gone. She took the cup with an unsteady hand and the tea slopped into the saucer like the lost plenty of happy times.

Nursing the teacup in her hands, she realised that Cowasjee was not really concentrating on the paper. His eyes moved restlessly from one news headline to the next as he flicked through the pages. He seemed distracted and went on spreading the marmalade on his toast long after the task was done, stopping only to begin a soft, persistent tapping on the empty eggshell with his spoon. Every so often he would glance surreptitiously at her before looking away quickly as if oblivious of her gaze.

Abba Mian had been the same. Whenever he was worried about her or Bhaiya or Nudrat, he too would betray his concern through the meaningless repetition of some inconsequential gesture. On the first day of her matriculation exam, when he had insisted on taking her to the examination centre himself, he must have gone through *The Times of India* at least fifty times without perhaps taking in fifty of the printed words. These pointless tokens of concern never failed to irritate her. She longed for him to show his feelings more tangibly. She wished he would hug her, hold her close to him, kiss her and pet her; tell her that he loved her. But he equated such explicit expressions of emotion with loss of dignity. 'Abba Mian, why were you so incomplete? Where did you learn this reserve? To love so deeply, to be so passionately sensitive to every emotional nuance of those whom you loved, and yet be unable to express your feelings to them? But perhaps you were not alone in this. Such rectitude was the characteristic of your generation.' Her own loneliness deepened at the thought. Perhaps Cowasjee too was like Abba Mian.

'Arré baba, stop this rustling bustling! How can you claim to understand anything in the newspaper like this? First he picks up one page, and then he picks up the next. Now go to your court. Do your picking up and putting down there, before the judge. I'm fed up with it. I haven't even had a chance to look at the headlines, and any minute now, Manuchehr will emerge; then *he'll* clutch the paper under his arm and disappear into the bathroom!' Mrs. Cowasjee concluded her diatribe and planted the tea cosy on the pot like a cap on the head of some hapless child.

Cowasjee got up in some confusion; folded the paper and placing it before Mrs. Cowasjee, left the dining room.

Mrs. Cowasjee picked it up and after casting a cursory glance at the front page, set it aside and began to clear the table. Birjees offered to help, but she rejected the offer and said, 'You'd better go now. Cowasjee is waiting. He has to go to court, but before he leaves he wants to pick your brain to bits yet again!'

Reluctantly Birjees went to the lounge. She had barely time to sit down before Cowasjee in his black lawyer's coat and tie, a bundle of files under his arm, entered the room. He placed the files on the harmonium, pulled up a chair to face her and sat down.

'I am going to court now, and will request you not to set off on another adventure while I'm away. I'm taking your passport with me—it is necessary to register your arrival in this country with the police.' He fell in to a brief silence, and then addressed her again, 'Did you think of asking the tenants in your relation's old house about their whereabouts? People often leave a forwarding address for the mail.'

'I did; but they had no further information. However, I did ask them for the address of the owner of the house. I felt that perhaps he would be able to direct me to them.'

'Well, that's the one intelligent thing you've done so far! What did he have to say?'

'I set out for his house after leaving my luggage with the new tenants, but some one misdirected me and I ended up here. Then it began to rain.'

Further enquiries by Cowasjee elicited the name and address of the landlord. It was a Mr. Masud Ahmad, owner of a residential guesthouse at Regal Square.

'I'll look up Mr. Masud Ahmad, but you, in the meantime, are not to set foot out of the house—and see if you can think of the names or addresses of some other relatives in this city,' then placing his spectacles on his nose, he arose, picked up his files and left the room.

It was a scene from a tale told by someone—or a clip from a film, an incident in some novel—beginning with last night and progressing to this moment, from her home to this place, a story of loss and separation, of distances and loneliness and then, more loneliness. Where would it all end? Pervaiz, Ashraf Chacha, Surriya—where had they all gone? She was lost in a labyrinth and the ones she was seeking had hidden themselves in the silence of the maze. Her heart was swept with desolation, eddies of arid dust blew across her face.

Her gaze fell on the harmonium and brought Kallu Maharaj to mind, how inextricably the two were linked. Her hand to her ear, she is sitting respectfully in front of him in the living room. One wrong note, and his anger erupts over her head; then spiralling coils of sound as his voice picks up the raag and fills the room. 'All right now, tell me the names of the ten musical arrangements?

'Ji Maharaj. They are Kalyan thaat, Bhairon thaat, Bhairveen thaat, Bilawal thaat ... she follows the arrangement established by Thakur Nawab Ali Khan and

Pandit Bhatkande. 'Now Beta, repeat the names of the four modes.

'Ji Maharaj. Adam Matt, Bharat Matt, Kal Nath Matt, Hanu Matt ...'

'Well done! Remember, Adam Matt is also known as the Shiv Matt and Kal Nath Matt also goes by the name of Krishan Matt.'

'Ji Maharaj,' she nods her head in respectful acquiescence.

Like everything else, the world of sound too is gendered. The raags Bhairon, Malkauns, Hindol, Deepak, Sri and Megh are male, while Bhairveen, Todi, Lalit, Kamud, and other sundry raagnis are female. Here there is a continuous reinvocation of the story of Eve's birth from Adam's rib. A confluence of looks between Brahma, Shiv and Vishnu brought forth Parwati just as raags gave birth to raagnis. The ten thaats contain six raags and these six have spawned thirty raagnis and much else besides, and all of them are bound up with time. If the morning raags are Gun Kalli, Bairagi and Jogia, the day lays claim to Bhairon, Bilawal and Balaas Khani. So too the late afternoon and evening, with their own raags, and then the different stages of the night, beginning with Bagaishari, Jai Jai Vanti, Darbari, Mian ki Malhar ending with Malkauns, ChandKauns and MudhKauns; all of them interwoven in an immense complexity. Here was the kinship of sound patterns, laying claim to their own castes and sub-castes, tribes, families; distinct, separate yet each twined with the other, all, inextricably linked through a myriad interconnections.

Bhairon is the jogi, with matted hair and body smeared with ash. An iron bangle encircles his wrist and in his aspect resides the glow of the new, unborn moon. Two snakes coil around his arm, the sandalwood mark is visible on his forehead and a rosary of skulls hangs around his neck as he meditates seated on a leopard skin under a tree in a verdant fold amidst mountains. Sindhi Prakash is the name of a raag to which Bhairon has given birth. It marks the meeting of light and dark, and is sung at dawn and dusk, the confluence of the night with the day and the day with the night.

She sings the alaap, the opening notes of the raag –

Sa—nee—dha—nee—sa—ray—sa

Sa—nee—dha—nee—sa—ray—sa

Nee—dha—pa –dha—nee—dha—ray—sa

Her voice falters and Kallu Maharaj's wrath descends on her head.

'Fling it away Beta! All the practice, all the hard work; take them and fling them in the kitchen fire!'

Kallu Maharaj, the best among music teachers, lives in Sabzi Bagh, and every day he is driven to their house at Bhanwar Pokhar, and after the music lesson, driven back again in the family's personal bicycle rickshaw. Shankar Bhaiya pedals the rickshaw and lives with his wife and children. Tucking his beeri behind his ear and hoisting up his dhoti to his knees, he pedals to an accompaniment of warning cries: 'Give way brother!' 'Mind your step, brother!' 'Look out!' Ferrying Kallu Maharaj to and fro is the bane of his life. The man must weight at least two and a half maunds. Once he settles in the rickshaw there isn't room to spare for two sesame seeds.

'Only Ram can tell when his funeral bier will go Mathura-wards!' he grumbles after depositing Kallu Maharaj at his house.

'You'll be canon-fodder, Shankar Bhaiya, if ever Kallu Maharaj hears you and reports you to Abba Mian.'

'Array Beta, it will be better to die once and be done with it than to face death every day! Hazoor can make a pancake out of me and fling me into the kitchen fire for all I care!' In his mind, there was little difference between a canon and the kitchen fire.

'But I ask you Beta, how long is this "ting-tong" of yours going to continue? You've been at that harmonium for years.'

'Not yet, Shankar Bhaiya, not yet! It will be another five to ten years before I'm through,' she would reply innocently and he would slap the seat of the rickshaw with his hand and walk huffily away to his hut.

A sudden shiver ran through her body. It was nine thirty in the morning—the time when she sat down to her riaz, the time set aside for her music practice, singing the raags and raagnis, matching komal with tewar, the high note with the low binding them together in a pattern of sound—the time for Balaas Khani, Shud Todi and Des—but where was her des? Her land? Where was Kallu Maharaj?

There were footsteps—Kallu Maharaj had come—she tried to get up—Mrs. Cowasjee was standing before her.

'Now why are you sitting here with your head down? Give your mind a rest for a little while! Don't worry! My Advocate General will nose out your relatives like a detective!' She sat down on the takht near the harmonium.

She was at a loss for words. Then, in a bid to break the silence, asked 'Who plays the harmonium?'

'This … this?' the colour fled from Mrs. Cowasjee's face. 'Nobody—since a long time. Do *you* play the harmonium?'

For a fleeting moment she thought of denying all knowledge of the instrument, but the words would speak themselves. She nodded her head in acquiescence.

'A long time has passed since it was played. I'm sure it needs tuning.' She tried to laugh but the salt of tears lurked beneath the smile. Birjees knew the signs. She had an intimate knowledge of this smile—so too had Abba Mian looked at times.

'Mama!' It was a young male voice that called.

'Now, my Prince of Wales has woken up. Now I will run this way and that! First he'll want one thing, then he'll want another!' The grumbled muttering was redolent with the fragrance of love and belonging. 'Let him shower and become human first, then I'll introduce him to you. He's a good doctor, but crazy! His father offered to set him up in his own clinic but he wants to serve humanity! His father said, go to London for an F.R.C.S—or M.R.C.P degree, but he doesn't want any of that. He wants to work in a free hospital.' The saga accompanied Mrs. Cowasjee out of the lounge.

Birjees walked across to the table bearing the piled boxes with the 'His Master's Voice' insignia. She lifted one lid to find records of Kamla Jhariya, Akhtari Bai Faizabadi, Sehgal and Shamshad Begum. The next box revealed a collection of instrumental music and the third, songs from the productions of Bombay theatrical companies. 'Rustum, Sohrab', 'Shirin, Khusrau' by the Zoroastrian Club, 'Sita Ban Baas' by the Atehak Naatak Mandal, Dad Bhai Thonti's 'Sitamgar'—the distance of hundreds of miles, a different culture and a different religion, another language and another life style—and yet, she continued to uncover bits and pieces of her own home in this house.

She picked up Sehgal's: *baalam ao basso moray man mein—beloved come dwell in my heart*. It had been a great favourite with Pervaiz. In the long summer afternoons when the khas chiks were sprayed with water and the hum of the high-ceilinged fans filled the rooms; when silence held the streets in thrall and the Loo wind stalked the streets with bared teeth, Pervaiz would usually come by to the house.

Abba Mian would drop her off at her college on his way to the courts in the morning, and in the summer afternoons, when Shankar Bhaiya came to fetch her, Pervaiz would often get in the rickshaw with her.

'Chhotti Ammi will be most disapproving when she sees you with me,' she would remind him.

'*I* find it very amusing, the way her face reddens and her nostrils twitch with anger. But I must say, yaar, your Chhotti Ammi is quite a looker!'

'Mind your tongue, Pervaiz; you're speaking of your aunt.' But his speech acknowledged no limits. It refused to recognize the social and familial boundaries that would impede its flow.

'Now that's a funny one! How does being my aunt stop her from being beautiful? You'll have to blindfold me—or paint her face with tar, if you want me not to say anything!'

'All right! All right! Now stop talking nonsense, Shankar Bhaiya can hear you.'

'So? You're threatening me with Shankar Bhaiya as if he were God'

'Yes, both God and Shankar Bhaiya can hear you.'

Bickering and squabbling, they would reach home, but before the rickshaw entered the porch, Pervaiz would leap out and walk into the house with a whistle on his lips. He would then pounce on Nudrat or Bhaiya, whoever happened to be there first, and swing them around. Chhotti Ammi couldn't stand him. If she could have had her way, she would have unsheathed one of the swords or daggers displayed on the baithak wall and run him through. But he was Abba Mian's brother's son, and his favourite nephew to boot, and she was shrewd enough never to let a word against him cross her lips.

He would be boisterous at the table and lunch would be a noisy meal. 'Kanizan Bua, where's the sweet tamarind chutney? What's the point of daal and rice without tamarind chutney?'

Chhotti Ammi's forehead would furrow with displeasure, 'Mian, why don't you ever make this kind of fuss with your mother?'

'Now, how can you even suggest such a thing? At my mother's table it is unheard of to sit down to a meal without at least four different kinds of pickles, chutneys and preserves,' he would retort, throwing a quick wink in Birjees' direction before busying himself with the meal.

On days when both tamarind chutney and raita graced the table he would demand citron preserve, 'Don't you know, in the hot weather citron preserve is essential with arhar beans, while limes and onions counter the effect of Loo. The hakims of old think that …'

'For God's sake Pervaiz, will you stop citing the hakims and philosophers at us,' she would burst out in exasperation. 'I'm not interested in their homilies!' She knew that once he had gone Chhotti Ammi's barbs would find her.

The meal done, he would still refuse to leave, and appear in her room with Nudrat and Bhaiya in tow.

'There is a hot Loo abroad—I'll get heatstroke if I go out now—who will look after you then?'

'You are not so fragile that the Loo will harm you. Even cholera and the plague won't come near you! Now out of my room, I'm sleepy. I have a test tomorrow and must work tonight.'

'And when am I stopping you from sleeping? Just turn on your side and nod off. I'm waiting for the kulfi walla; then the three of us will have kulfi, right?' and the children would shout in agreement. 'All right then, Nudrat and Bhaiya, now begins our musical request programme,' he would continue settling down near her radiogram, and soon the room would echo to Sehgal's 'beloved come dwell in my heart.'

'Turn that thing off!'

'Why? He has a beautiful voice?'

'It may be a beautiful voice, but what business has a man, to address a male beloved?'

'But what is your objection?'

'A strong one! Why can't he address the female beloved? It's ridiculous of him to take on the female persona in his song!'

'Okay, if you don't like the words of this song on a man's lips, why don't you rectify the error and sing it yourself? It is in the fitness of things that a love-lorn girl should sing to her beloved and ask him to come dwell in her heart.'

At this point she would hurl her pillows and books at him and he, along with Nudrat and Bhaiya, would beat a hasty retreat.

'Birjees!' Mrs. Cowasjee's voice fell on her ears and the dream fled.

She peeped into the dining room and saw a slim young man busy with his breakfast. He stood up on seeing her; there was no hint of suspicion in the intelligent eyes that looked at her from behind a pair of spectacles. She observed him carefully, a white shirt, white cotton trousers a brown tie and a face that was both grave and gentle. So this was

Manuchehr, who had studied medicine and instead of making money and going to London for a higher degree wanted to serve humanity.

Silence fell in the room after the exchange of routine greetings.

'Birjees darling, don't mind my son. He is like the dumb, he measures each word with an inch tape before uttering it,' Mrs. Cowasjee commented candidly and a flush mounted Manuchehr's pale face. Embarrassed, he cast her a fleeting glance then pushed aside a half finished cup of tea and got up from the table. 'I must go. It's getting late, please excuse me.'

'Now we'll not see his face till nightfall. There is never a time when he comes home for lunch—so many times I've told him to take his lunch with him—but will he listen to one word? All that matters is his patients and him!' complained Mrs. Cowasjee, raising her voice, she called out, 'Halima Bai! Ay Halima Bai!'

'Coming Bai, coming!' came a voice from the kitchen and a middle aged woman, dressed in an ankle length cotton kurta and loose, straight pyjamas, entered the room and having greeted Birjees, began to clear the table.

'Bai, is she one of your relatives?'

'No, she has come from India.'

'From India?' her eyes lit up, 'is she from Meenu Bai's in-laws then?'

The smile was wiped off Mrs. Cowasjee's face. 'You look to your work Bai,' she chided roughly. The harsh tone took Birjees by surprise. 'Get up Birjees. Halima Bai will see to the kitchen and we'll relax for a while. Do you play cards?'

'Yes.'

'Then we'll have a game. Go into the lounge while I get the cards.'

Birjees went and sat in the lounge and after a few minutes Mrs. Cowasjee, laden with cushions and a pack of cards in her hand, joined her. Settling down on the takht near the harmonium, she asked her to shuffle the cards. 'Now remember, no cheating1'

Birjees smiled and leaned back against the cushion.

Halima Bai served lunch, and the meal done, Mrs. Cowasjee retired to her bedroom with injunctions to Birjees to take her afternoon nap. Too churned up to follow her instructions, she stepped out on the balcony. Overcome with uncertainty and a sense of her own helplessness, rest was the last thing she could contemplate. Leaning against the railing, she looked down at the unending flow of bicycle-rickshaws, motor cars, taxis, pedestrians; constantly on the move, ever-shifting, changing, the street was a world unto itself. Tired of watching the traffic she returned to the lounge and lay down on the takht. Her fingers stroked the silent harmonium and the notes that yearned for a voice in each pore of her body, remained mute. With what pains had she wrested permission from Abba Mian to learn music. Nor had Chhotti Ammi been sparing of her taunts: 'The daughter of a respectable house with the tastes of a courtesan!' she had sneered. The words had drawn blood, but she had swallowed the insult in silence. She knew that one word in Abba Mian's ear would seal her stepmother's fate, leaving her to bewail her fortune for the rest of her days, but she had no desire to wreck her father's home, nor could she contemplate separation from Nudrat and Bhaiya.

Pervaiz was another one who felt a fortuitous hatred for her music, especially now, when her programme was being broadcast from Patna Radio. If he happened to be there during her music lessons, he would enquire sarcastically, 'where did you acquire the predilections of itinerant entertainers and mirasans?'

'Is that how you view Roshan Ara Begum and Akhtari Bai Faizabadi? As mirasans and itinerant entertainers?' she would retort sharply.

'By the Grace of God, we have a female Tansen in our midst! Spring has been glorified already by Roshan Ara Begum's songs, now we have you to elevate it further!'

'Yes! Do you mind?'

'When your illustrious father does not mind, who am I among a long line of contenders, to raise objections?'

'You are offensive. Don't forget that my father happens to be your uncle!'

'You too should not forget that you are my affianced wife. My mother claimed you for me at birth.'

At this point she would walk away angrily. She knew that in a little while his anger would blow over and he would hover around her again. Pervaiz was very dear to her, but some of his ideas repelled her.

The sound of footsteps made her raise her head from the cushion. It was Halima Bai.

'Bai hides things from me; she won't tell me you are one of Meenu Bai's in-laws. How is it with her? Is she well and happy? Does she ever remember her home?' She looked expectantly at Birjees, sure of an answer, confounding her and leaving her at a loss for a reply. She had no idea who Halima Bai had mistaken her for, nor could she fathom why Mrs. Cowasjee had scolded her earlier. Unsure of what to say, she parried the question: 'You care very much for Meenu Bai, don't you?'

'She was a good girl, caring for every little need of mine. When my daughter got married, she gave a present, helped out with household goods and came to Marwari Lane to attend the wedding. She gave me much honour among my kin and my people.' She wiped her eyes with the corner of her coarse muslin dupatta, 'does she have any children? A little boy or a girl? Or does she still go about with empty hands?'

'Halima Bai, I don't know any Meenu Bai,' she replied at last.

'You have come to Cowasjee's house, and you don't know his daughter? How is that possible?' Halima Bai looked at her in disbelief. 'Her going away made us all poor. Her mother and father became poor. She talked! She laughed! She sang! Who could have imagined that she would do this to us?' She drew a deep breath.

'Why? What did she do?' by now Birjees' curiosity had been aroused.

'Array Bai, it was Advani Sa'ab who lived on the second floor. Meenu Bai wanted to marry his boy, Rattan. Then the country was divided and Advani Sa'ab left and his boy Rattan left. Meenu Bai wrote letters to him and Cowasjee found out and made a big noise. He said, "My community will excommunicate me! My friends will leave me; my way of life will be finished!" My Bai argued and argued with her, but she could make no dent in Meenu Bai's head. She understood nothing! Then one day she left, taking only a few clothes with her and Cowasjee grew old in a day. That boy had cast a spell on her—she was like one in thrall—that is why my Bai, who was as beautiful as a heifer, left us and went away.'

Halima Bai was carried away by the trajectory of her tale and at each turn in the narrative, veils lifted from Birjees' eyes. Cowasjee's sternness last night; the way he had scolded her that morning just like Abba Mian; the sheen of tears in Mrs. Cowasjee's smile—it all made sense now.

Cowasjee came home in the evening and even before he had taken his first sip of tea, he returned her passport to her, 'your arrival has been registered with the police. Take it and keep it safe.'

The bad news was that Masud Ahmad, the owner of the Residential Guest House Hotel, who might have guided them to Ashraf Chacha, was away in England and would not be back for a month. The ground seemed to move beneath her feet; she felt she was marooned on a sinking ship. Cowasjee shot a glance at her ashen face and said, 'the trouble with your kind is that you act first and think afterwards. You're all selfish. You are blind to everything but your own immediate needs! You will now come with us and collect your stuff from where you've left it—which reminds me, have you been able to remember the names and addresses of some other relatives in this city?'

'No!' her reply was barely audible.

'Then the only option left to you is to go back.'

'I beg your pardon?' She gave him a startled look.

'The people you have come in search of have moved away, the man who could have guided us to them is away, *you* do not know of any other relations in this city. Now you tell me, what option do you have but to turn back?'

'That is the one thing I cannot do. I cannot go back.'

'And why can't you go back? Isn't it better to return home and be accountable to your family instead of running from pillar to post in a strange city? I cannot believe that you undertook such a long journey alone and unaccompanied with the permission of your family. I am sure you are hiding something from us!' Stern and unrelenting, Cowasjee stood there with his hands clasped behind his back.

The echoes of his daughter's story still lingered in Birjees' ears, she was sure that he was weighing her and Meenu on the same scales.

'I cannot go back!' she was close to tears. 'There must be a Y.W.C.A hostel here. I'll take a room there and continue to search for my family.'

'Don't be silly!'

'Now why are you making such a noise? Standing there and prosecuting her like that! Baba, a girl's heart is fragile like glass, speak gently to her.' Mrs. Cowasjee glared at her husband. 'It was this hasty talk of yours that destroyed our family. You live on a diet of grass instead of lunch and dinner!' Giving her an angry look, Cowasjee walked out of the room.

She placed a comforting hand on her shoulder, 'don't you worry Birjees. Cowasjee's mind has become a merry-go-round. Now go and change, I'll go with you.'

'Go where?' nothing seemed to make sense to her anymore.

'Array baba! What kind of a girl are you? Didn't Cowasjee tell you just now? To the place where you left your luggage—that's where!'

Moving like an automaton she arose, took out her last suit of clothes from the bag, ironed it, washed, changed and returned to the lounge. A few minutes later, accompanied by Mr. and Mrs. Cowasjee she descended the same stairs where she had sought shelter only twenty-four hours earlier.

Cowasjee's Morris entered P.I.B Colony, turning left and right into the smaller streets as he read out the house numbers. Seated on mundhas outside their front doors, groups of people stared curiously as they drove past. It did not take them long to find the house; Cowasjee rang the doorbell as Birjees and Mrs. Cowasjee got out of the car. The old woman's bad-tempered husband—the one who had initially refused to let her leave her suitcase there—answered the door. He stared at the three of them for a few minutes before he recognized Birjees, then cleared his throat loudly and shut the door only to return a moment later to lead them into a small room that did duty as baithak.

'And may I ask what your relationship is to this young lady?' he asked perching cautiously on a mundha. The eyes, sharp behind the spectacles, took close survey of Cowasjee as he spoke.

'I am a friend of her father. She sent a telegram informing her uncle and myself of her arrival, but it was late in reaching us. She had a lot of difficulty in getting to our house.'

'It is a world turned upside down—the very foundations are awry and nothing is as it should be. We are stumbling in darkness and anarchy rules! This young lady turned up here, unceremoniously roaming the streets with nothing but her face to accompany her, looking for her uncle's house. Why did she not think of informing them in time of her arrival dates?' The stiff inflection of 'young lady' accompanied by a shake of the head left little room for doubt about the tenor of his thoughts.

'Come Sir, do you think it possible that her family would have failed to apprise us of her plans? They gave us of the date of her arrival in Lahore—but you know how things are here—everything is in a state of disorder—but tell me, have *you* any idea of Ashraf sahib's whereabouts? Surely he must've had some contacts in the neighbourhood. He must've left a forwarding address with someone?'

'What can I say? From what one hears, it seems that the move came without warning. They left at night and their only response to the neighbours was that they had found this house cramped and had taken a more spacious apartment.

As far as the new address was concerned, Ashraf sahib could remember neither the name of the street nor the house number. But he would be back he said, not only with the exact address but to take them with him to show them the new house—and that was the last time that anyone here heard from him.' The tassel on the old man's Turkish cap kept time with the movement of his head— 'Yesterday, after this young lady's departure, I said to my householder, "Good woman, go ask the neighbours if they have any news"—and go she did, but got the same answer everywhere—nobody had any information to give.'

But how was this possible? Ashraf Chacha was a gregarious soul, happy to meet people, happy to share their joys and sorrows. Even if it were not possible for him to be widely known in the community, surely there must have been a few homes where he had been on calling terms? And then there was Surriya with her knack of making friends! How was it that nobody knew where they had gone?

'Aji can you hear me?' A voice called from behind a closed wooden door, and the old man leapt up and went inside.

Birjees was certain that from the hidden cracks and crannies in the house, the old man's pale, repressed daughters were peering at them in wonderment.

The old man emerged from behind the closed door bearing a rusty tin tray sloshing over with cups of tea. Close behind him came an elderly woman, her face veiled by a dyed muslin dupatta. She sat down with her back turned carefully towards Cowasjee. There were blackened silver bangles on her wrists and cheap tarnished gold rings on her fingers. The old man served them tea.

Addressing the air in front of her, the old crone spoke, 'Array Bibi, my heart has been in turmoil since she left yesterday. An unknown city and a girl alone—where could she have gone, how would she pass the night?

But I must say she has guts. My girls would be afraid to step into the street, and here this one has travelled all these hundreds of miles on her own! Well done, Beta, well done!' and she stroked Birjees' back in a show of approval.

She was convinced that the old woman's stomach was churning with curiosity. There was nothing in Mrs. Cowasjee's style and bearing that fitted with Birjees' cultural background. There was no visible connection between the two and this difference, she was sure, must rankle in those flint-sharp eyes.

'You're right! I was horrified when she turned up suddenly like that,' Mrs. Cowasjee took up and reinforced the narrative begun by her husband.

Cowasjee and the Barre Mian were conversing in low tones. The Barri Bi sat silently for a few moments, then unable to restrain herself any longer, bent forward towards Birjees to enquire conspiratorially, 'She is not from amongst us, is she?'

'No! She is not,' she replied briefly.

'She looks a little like a mem; but then, she isn't dressed like one?'

'You could say she is a bit of both.' she was embarrassed by this whispered confabulation and the ferreting was getting on her nerves. Sensing disapproval, Barri Bi changed tack—'and have you managed to find out anything about your uncle's whereabouts then?'

'No, but I'm sure uncle will find him.' She glanced at Cowasjee who, having taken a couple of sips of the cold, vapid tea looked at her signalling his desire to leave.

'About my luggage ...' she put down her cup and an itinerant mosquito zoomed to a watery death.

'Wait a bit Beta, both your cases are as you left them. After all, what right have we to another's belongings? I assure you, nobody has so much as touched them!—Aji I am asking you, will you take out the cases and have them put in the car—yes, as I was saying Beta, wait a minute while the cases are taken out—it'll take a bit of time— rheumatism has made him quite helpless. Before he fell prey to these aches and pains there was his sole self and all the work in the neighbourhood. It was the evil eye of the accursed ones that got him! How can I tell you how much work he did? Oh, how busy he used to be! I would like to ask those God-forsaken ones, when the very thought of work makes you act as if you'd been orphaned, why do you crib when others take responsibility for it? What am I to tell you Beta, it was envy that got him!' Supporting her weight on her knees with both hands she got up and Birjees and Mrs. Cowasjee shook their heads in an expression of sympathy. Pulling her ghunghat further down on her face, her back still turned carefully towards Cowasjee, Barri Bi exited crab-like from the room.

The cases, which had been dragged into the tiny courtyard, were placed in the boot of the car with the joint efforts of both men, and they drove off amidst protestations of gratitude and appreciation.

The wheels of the car ate up the miles, swallowed up distances. Caught intermittently in the headlights of oncoming vehicles, the moments shone briefly like stars, but there was nothing to break the silence inside the car. It was as if all the words in the world had been used up and the voices that were their birthright, lost forever.

Cowasjee parked the car in the compound and went in search of the chowkidar.

'Come Birjees, let us go up. Cowasjee will see to the luggage.' Taking her by the hand, Mrs. Cowasjee drew her towards the stairs.

She shivered as she climbed the stairs. It was on these very steps last night that the sky had wept with her. It was on one of these treads that Mrs. Cowasjee had dropped her brooch. What if the brooch hadn't been lost—or having been lost—she hadn't found it—what would have happened then? So many 'ifs'! May be that was what life was about—an aggregate of random, meaningless 'ifs'. Yet each 'if' was replete with dire possibility—each one containing an endlessly unravelling saga of dread before which one was abjectly powerless—over which one had no control.

Later that night Cowasjee again brought up the question of her return.

'Your decision to come here was made unthinkingly and in haste without even the precaution of discovering the address of some other relative before you set out. This was foolishness on your part. It is only right that you should now return to your family. If, unlike countless Muslims who are staying on, you still don't want to live in India, you can come back at a later time,' he argued.

'I didn't want to come—but when there was no home left for me to stay in –' Birjees took a deep breath and then, without reservation—hiding and withholding nothing— unfolded her tale to the two unknown yet sympathetic listeners.

When she finished, Mrs. Cowasjee left her chair to come and sit near her and her hand reached out to clasp her arm. Cowasjee, who seemed to be searching for something in the fate lines of his hand, looked up and said, 'I will find a way to trace your uncle. But until that happens, you will stay with us. Think of this as your father's house in Karachi.' He left the room swiftly; his eyes were wet with tears.

Mrs. Cowasjee kissed her forehead, 'Now you stay here for a while. I'm going to give Manuchehr his dinner and then I'll come back and make up your bed. Tonight you will sleep in this room.'

But healing sleep forsook her eyes, and when thoughts of bygone days had exhausted her weary brain, she came out onto the balcony. The silence of the night stretched around her. Steeped in narratives of loss and separation, the tired light of the waning moon slept on the trees and fell on somnolent walls and empty doorways. It was then, in that alien city, that the image of home arose before her eyes and the whole register of accounts unfolded page by page.

Abba Mian, why were you in such a hurry to go? This impatience, this feverish haste—they were not part of your nature. Now that you are one with the dust, do you have any idea that you're going turned my life to ashes? All supports, all choices have been snatched away from me …

How happy Abba Mian had been at her graduation. He had wanted her to study Law, but her heart had been set on English Literature and a Masters from Lucknow University. He had tried to dissuade her, but she had been adamant and his arguments had been in vain. Chhotti Ammi had shot a few barbs at her and Pervaiz had first looked disapproving and then scolded her, but fed up with the circumlocutions of domestic politics, she had gone her own way.

Chhotti Ammi had many faces and the one she wore before Abba Mian was different from the one she revealed in his absence. At birth Birjees had been promised to Pervaiz but Chhotti Ammi disapproved of the match. She never voiced her opinion openly, but secretly she plotted and planned all the time. Birjees loved Pervaiz, but kept her feelings hidden, and now she had begun to fear her stepmother. It was this realization that led to her decision to study in another city. She felt that once removed from her stepmother's presence she would cease to rankle in her eyes.

When the time had come for her to go to Lucknow, Abba Mian himself had accompanied her there and had seen her settled in Kailash hostel. Hazrat Ganj, Qaiser Bagh, Gumti, the University, the Radio Station, name, status, place—for an instant she was shaken by a flood of memories. How carefree had been those days and how heedless the nights. She had missed Abba Mian, Nudrat and Bhaiya, and Pervaiz was constantly in her thoughts, but their absence was untouched by sadness. There was only the waiting and the pleasurable anticipation of reunion. After all, it was only a question of two years; these would speed by and then all distances would be obliterated. Full of complaints and grievances, Pervaiz's letters would arrive, making her double over with laughter. Letters from Abba Mian and Nudrat brought with them the fragrance of love, while Bhaiya, who was still learning to write, drew pictures in his childish hand, scrawled his name on them and sent them to her.

On her return home for the summer break, Abba Mian's love had driven her to distraction, hemming her in to the extent that it became a problem to visit friends or spend time with Pervaiz, but even in these constraints there was an element of pleasure. And in any case visits from Pervaiz had become a bit of a rarity.

The holidays drew to a close and she returned to Lucknow. Hardly a few weeks of the final term had gone by when the telegram arrived bringing news of Abba Mian's illness. Afraid and with reddened eyes she had rushed home, but her father, who had never in her life denied her anything, turned a deaf ear to her entreaties and went quietly to sleep. After the fitful wakefulness of a long night he finally found repose at the break of day.

About her mother she had heard a lot but could remember nothing. She knew her only through her photographs—a smiling face and a girl beneath a haar singhaar tree gazing at some distant perspective, or seated in an armchair in the verandah with a few beautifully bound books on a small table beside her and a few snapshots with a youthful looking Abba Mian. There were others in which she featured as well—seated in her mother's lap or playing on the carpet. But Birjees could never think of that young girl as her mother. She thought of her as an older sister or even a friend—her friends' mothers had greying hair and faces that showed signs of age—but this was the face of a young girl—a happy, carefree girl who had left her and Abba Mian to sleep in the family graveyard.

She had heard that for years she had been the only person with whom Abba Mian was seen to smile; that everyday he spent hours at her mother's grave. That was the time he had transformed the cemetery into a flower garden. His second marriage had taken place many years after his wife's death.

He had given her so much love, so much care that she had never felt the need of a mother. For the first eight or nine years of her life he had seen to her every need himself. Every night she drifted off to sleep to the sound of Abba Mian's bedtime stories and every morning she had awoken to the sound of his voice.

When this gentle, loving father, who had fulfilled her every wish, left her and went away, she was engulfed in a silence so deep and dense that even the sound of Pervaiz's voice failed to pierce it. The home, which had been hers in her father's lifetime, vanished with him. Chhotti Ammi's nieces and nephews who used to call only on Eid or Bakr-Eid to sit formally in the drawing room and leave after receiving their Eidi, could now be seen milling around the house at all hours. On the tenth day after her father's death Chacha Roshan Rai told her that the house had been left to her stepmother while she, Nudrat and Bhaiya had shares in the family business. Two orchards had also been left in her name along with seven thousand rupees in her bank account. She listened to him with bowed head. All that she knew was that her father was dead. That was the only reality. The rest did not matter.

On the twentieth day after Abba Mian's death she returned to Lucknow. Chhotti Ammi tried her best to stop her from going, but her taunts and barbs had lost their power to hurt. She knew that now, as never before she needed her MA degree. Pervaiz had been writing around applying for jobs for some time now, but to no avail. Once she completed her Masters there was a chance that she at least would be eligible for a job as a college lecturer. Then, married, the two would manage life's business somehow.

A couple of months after reaching Lucknow she heard from Pervaiz's younger sister who was also her closest friend. Surriya had written … 'you will find it hard to believe but my father and brother have decided to move to Pakistan.

The house and the orchard have already been sold and we will be leaving Patna within the next day or two.'

She found it hard to credit this news.

Was it possible that Pervaiz could take such a major decision about his life without consulting her? But whether she believed it or not, that was exactly what he had done. Nor had he thought it worth his while to inform her of his decision. The realization intensified life's loneliness by a few more degrees.

Pervaiz's letter reached her some weeks later. It had been posted in Karachi. 'I have come here,' he wrote, 'I had longed to meet you before leaving, but I feared were I to do so, I would perhaps be compelled to change my decision. This I could not afford to do, especially now when it has become virtually impossible for Muslims to find jobs in India. That is why I behaved so cruelly with you and myself. I want to achieve something as quickly as possible so that I can ask you to join me. In any case there are now only a few months to go before you take your exam. Time is short and life is difficult.'

The letter raised a storm of protest in her heart. Apart from being first cousins, their mothers had been friends. If the tales told by the mamas and maidservants were to be believed, they were inseparable and happiest when together. And then, Ashraf Chacha and Abba Mian were first cousins and they too had been close to each other. It had come as no surprise when, at her birth Pervaiz's mother had claimed her for her son with a silver coin and the shard of a clay pot. The family had been delighted; everyone felt that now these bonds of love would grow stronger.

Pervaiz was a part of her first conscious memories and the two along with his sister Surriya grew up as playmates. And now when Abba Mian was no longer there, he had taken such a major decision without even consulting her. She had never dreamed that she would live anywhere except in her own land. At the time of Partition, when so many had made ready for the long trek to the new country, Abba Mian had only one thing to say, 'Mian, this dust is our mother. It is the leaven in our blood and we can sleep peacefully only on its breast. You will never find peace away from it.' With this rejoinder he would settle his Gandhi cap more firmly on his head and look with sadness at each departing back as if he was attending a funeral.

And now, without a word, without a sign, ignoring the living and casting aside the claims of the dead, Abba Mian's own prospective son-in-law had gone away. Judge Dawar Ali Khan was no more and with him had gone his status and privileged position. The wall that had stood between Pervaiz and Pakistan crumbled. Surriya's letters reached her with great regularity; Pervaiz's letters though infrequent were full of shared memories and promises about the future.

Birjees sat for her last paper and left Lucknow for Patna to find that her home had become a house. Bewildered, she roamed from room to room, searching for a sense of her father's presence among his clothes and books. Chhotti

Ammi's taunts were sharper and Nudrat and Bhaiya subdued and awkward in her company. The study was deserted and the phaeton had been sold and Sitara and Jai Mangal had moved to Barrister Pankhaj Singh's stables. Driven by unemployment Nassu Khan had set his face towards his village and Naju Chacha had been told to leave.

She continued to walk the tightrope of a graceless existence till one night Chhotti Ammi baldly announced her decision to move to her parents' house at Hazari Bagh where she hoped to spend her remaining days with her family. The Bhanwar Pokhar house was up for sale and the search was on for buyers.

She listened in growing disbelief, but when she opened her mouth to speak, Chhotti Ammi cut her short: 'This house is in my name to live in, sell or set on fire if I please. In any case, you have nothing to worry about. Judge Sahib enabled you first to take your BA and then your MA, and there is all of Pakistan for you to live in. Take my advice and make your home with your Ashraf Chacha.'

There was no room for further speech. Her stepmother's words had sealed her lips. Many families were surreptitiously selling their household goods in readiness for the move to Pakistan but Judge Dawar Ali's family heirlooms were sold openly and in broad daylight. Maybe this was because Chhotti Ammi hated them. The car had been sent to Hazari Bagh on her arrival. Perhaps she feared that Birjees would fly around the city in it. The rickshaw was sold in front of her and Shankar Bhaiya turned out of his quarters. His protestations and cries mingled with those of his family were more than she could bear. That day, for the first time in her life in her own city, she took a hired rickshaw to go to her friend Nirmala's house where she broke down and wept.

Her faculties were numbed and the ability to think or even understand what was happening deserted her. Where was she to go? With whom could she find a home? All close relatives had left for Pakistan, and shorn of status and security the few who remained were leading a precarious life. She knew she was promised to Pervaiz—that one day they would wed—but to turn up thus unceremoniously at his family's doorstep, was neither seemly nor desirable.

Unable to find a solution to her predicament she had gone to Roshan Chacha's house. A retired judge, he was one of her father's closest friends. A connoisseur of Urdu and Persian poetry whose life had centred on the courtly phrases and aesthetic rituals of Urdu culture, he had lived to see his only son join the nationalist organisation, the Hindu Mahasabha. Birjees poured out her woes in his astounded though sympathetic ears. Shocked and grieving, Chaachi had embraced her and told her to pack up her things and move in with them, and Roshan Chacha had added his voice to hers. But Birjees knew that could not be. The world had changed and the balance had tilted in favour of the Mahasabhahis. Roshan Chacha and Chaachi had been relegated to the margins of the new world.

'I would have been the last man to tell Dawar Ali's daughter to go to Pakistan, but beta, the wind has shifted and it no longer blows with us. Now only Ashraf Mian can give you protection.'

Every breath had become painful, each moment a hell—was she then to leave the land which was her birthright just because Pervaiz had left it? Or was she to be driven out because of Chhotti Ammi's hatred? She thought of many options, made a hundred different plans only to reject each one in turn; they were all built on sand and crumbled at the touch. Perhaps that was why even on the day that her results were announced, she had stolen away from all thoughts of Abba Mian; the next day had brought a brief letter from Surriya. She had written: now that things have come to this pass, it is best that you should come to us. It seemed that news of her situation had trickled through to Pakistan: hence these few hasty lines.

In the unending tussle between desire and possibility, reality is always the winner and the long night of decision-making ended predictably. The next day she had completed her passport application forms and written briefly to Surriya, telling her that she would soon be with them.

Possessions that have grown dear become meaningless when faced with the exigencies of time. Her room was full of the treasured accumulations of the years, yet when she left it was only with two suitcases. And it was with this sum total of her life that she moved into Roshan Chacha's house where, despite his hatred for her, his Mahasabhahi son was compelled to tolerate her presence—just as Chhotti Ammi had been compelled to do during Abba Mian's lifetime.

Thus do love and hatred impose their constraints on the living breath.

She bade farewell to the mound of earth beneath which her father lay and began her journey away from the land that had given her everything.

The floodtide of memories swept her along till the very keenness of loss cast her back into the present. Her clothes, the balcony railing, the street below were drenched with dew; the dim moonlight fell on a cat soft-footing its slow way along the footpath. It reminded her of the cat her stepmother had hated and who, by her orders was routinely put in a sack and cast away somewhere far away, but who always made its way back to the house after an absence of a few days. Then Pervaiz had tied a piece of magnet around its neck and said: 'Don't worry Chachi, this time it won't come back.' He had claimed that the influence of the magnet's rays would make it lose its bearings and it would be unable to find its way home. For weeks she had waited for the cat's return but it never came back.

The next day Mrs. Cowasjee placed a burning ember of frankincense in a small afarzan and carried it from room to room till the house was radiant with the purifying influence of the sacred fire.

She was glancing through the morning paper after breakfast when Mrs. Cowasjee called out to her, telling her that Cowasjee was waiting for her in the study. The moment she stepped into the room, she was overcome by a faint dizziness. The particular smell of leather bound books and files, the large desk with its covering of green baize beneath the glass, the table lamp and Cowasjee in a rattan swivel chair were all part of the past. Responding to a gestured command she pulled up a chair and sat down. Cowasjee's figure wavered and dissolved in the air and Abba Mian's eyes looked at her through gold-rimmed spectacles as he pushed a piece of paper towards her. Startled, she glanced at its concise message: 'Birjees, daughter of the late Justice Dawar Ali Khan of Patna has arrived in Karachi. Her relations are requested to contact her at the following telephone number and address '

'I'm going to place this advertisement in *Dawn* and *Jang*. This is the only way I can think of for contacting your uncle.'

Birjees nodded in agreement. She was struck by the perverse humour of the situation that compelled her to look for Pervaiz through a newspaper advertisement. Had there been newspapers in Majnun's day they too would have been full of advertisements for bi Laila. Suddenly she was furious with Surriya and Pervaiz. How pressing after all could the claims on their time be that they had forgotten to inform her of their change of address? Admittedly the telegram had gone astray, yet they had been aware of her travel plans weeks before they moved house.

Cowasjee left for the court, Halima arrived and Mrs. Cowasjee got busy with housework. Birjees read the paper from end to end. Now what was she to do? How was she to fill in the empty hours? She thought of the old women who whiled away the day endlessly cutting betelnut, what better way than that to pass time? Pass time, pastime? Time too was passing, whittling away their days, nibbling relentlessly at decades, centuries, eons. When the last human life had been eaten away and Time itself ran out of time, what happened then? Did it start all over again counting back to zero?

She was still entangled in numbers when settling her pallu on her shoulder, Mrs. Cowasjee bustled in. 'Come, let me show you your room.'

'My room?'

'What do you think, that tomorrow the advertisement will appear in the papers and within ten minutes your relatives will arrive. Arré baba, it will take a day or two for them to get in touch, and will you continue to sit on the footpath till then? I have prepared your room for you and Halima Bai has taken your suitcases there. Come now, go there and rest a little.' Taking her by the hand, she took her to the room.

It opened on a balcony. The window curtains billowed in the breeze and a golden light suffused each corner and each object that lay there. There was not a speck of dust on the teak wood dressing table and bed, the Chinese vase was home to the brilliant blue of Argus-eyed peacock feathers and the framed print with its illustrated borders of calligraphic verses from the *Shahnama* depicted the lovelorn Manish's quest for Bezhan across the desert of loss. Yet, despite the high sheen of the mirrored surfaces a faint smell of the imprisoned air of disuse still clung to the walls.

The verses from the *Shahnama* had been Abba Mian's favourites. With Birjees' hand tucked securely in his, he would hum them on moonlit walks beneath ancient trees along the bank of the Ganga where steps led down to the river:

'Manizha munim dukht Afrasiyab, barhana na dida tunam aftab kunun dida pur khoon-o-dil pur zadard azeen dar badaan ...

I, Manizha, daughter of the great Afrasiyab, who was not seen unveiled by the sun, I was dragged naked to the pit of Bizhan. He is dragged down by chains; the helpless man's clothes are soaked in his blood. Because of my anxiety for him my eyes are filled with tears.

It struck her that this was Meenu's room. She stared at the framed print. Depicted there was Meenu's own story. She felt oppressed. Pain flared up in her heart, beating its wings against the confines of the flesh, then she realised that Mrs. Cowasjee was standing there awaiting her response. Pulling herself together she turned towards her: 'What a lovely room.'

The sheen of tears lay beneath her smile: 'Now rest', she said and hurried out of the room. The mother's torment had made deeper inroads in the depths of the heart than the father's grief and blurred the distinction between the smile and the tears.

Slowly Birjees walked to the bed. After a while she slipped off her chappals, drew up her feet and stretched out. Her back found comfort in its softness and her head sought refuge on the pillow.

That evening her hosts drove her to the beach. She climbed the yellow brick steps of Jehangir Kothari Parade Pavilion and standing beneath its yellow dome saw the red disc of the sun quench itself in the waters of the Arabian Sea. She was reminded of the hiss of burning embers when water is splashed on them and they turn from red to ashen pink and grey. But the sun, like the heart when it dies, slipped silently into the waters and lost its light.

Pervaiz, Surriya, Ashraf Chacha must all have come here. They had been in Karachi for a long time now; they must have come down to the sea at least once. She wondered where among the countless grains of sand the imprints of Pervaiz' feet were to be found? The very absurdity of the idea made her smile. Stemming from the clichéd discourse of devdasis and subservient conjugality of ancient tradition, such a thought could only merit laughter. Admitted that I love you dearly, yet I never lived by the air you breathed, nor felt that my actions owed their life to your behests. Nobody guessed my feelings for you. For those who saw us, my behaviour merely corroborated the fact that we were two people who had been promised to each other as children, that ours was a relationship forged by the claims of others—by the silver coin with which your mother crossed the midwife's palm when I was born. She gave a deep sigh.

Ours was not an easy relationship my friend and relationships born of such conflicting emotions should not vanish so easily in thin air. Surely the moments of friendship, the love, the quarrels and reconciliations merit remembrance? She continued to walk behind Mr. and Mrs. Cowasjee and Pervaiz' memory walked beside her, played with her hair and clung to her body.

Birjees belonged to the land of rivers, to the Ganga and the Jamuna; to the wide-flowing stream of the Soan, and the waters of the Gumti, the Ghaagar, the Gandak. The journey from Lahore to Karachi brought her face to face with rivers she knew only from geography books, but the sea was a different entity altogether. Rivers are fearsome only in times of flood when their banks can no longer contain their turbulence and they sweep over the habitations of men destroying all that lies in their path. But nothing can match the benignity of their aspect in normal times and that very calm tempts one to lay ones head on their breast; lose oneself in their waves. But the sea is always the same, awesome, terrible, infinite. She owed her acquaintance with the sea to English Literature—more specifically to Byron's 'Childe Harold'—and had learnt to regard it as a familiar friend, but now as she stood there counting its waves, it confronted her like a stranger, unknown and alienating.

She saw many Parsi couples by the seashore; walking on the beach, sitting silently on the stone benches looking into space. Alive, sentient yet already marked by the shadow of the Tower of Silence.

Returning from the beach they stopped for dinner at the Karachi Gymkhana. Cowasjee's flat was only a stone's throw away from the club under whose colonial façade the rituals of the Raj were still maintained. Silent soft-footed waiters in starched white served the sahibs, and elegantly dressed women tinkled with laughter and gossip.

Thin, finely shaped eyebrows were raised enquiringly at Birjees and a few voiced their interest in her identity.

'The daughter of an old and very dear friend,' replied Mrs. Cowasjee putting an end to further questions by placing the napkin on her lap and addressing herself to the soup.

Time too was partaking of its feast as peoples and communities scattered and its sharp teeth reshaped the geography of nations.

The dawn of the new day brought with it the daily ritual of the sacred fire and the fumes of frankincense filled the rooms. The ancient goddess of Mrs. Cowasjee's faith, the sacred fire had accepted offerings of sandalwood, deodar, fragrant herbs and animal fat. Child of the life-giving sun, symbol of truth and light it called to sinners and saints alike, asking for repentance and offering absolution from error and sin. Fire: seventh among the created elements, it had infused the other six with its influence. Humankind too had been born of the white and gold flames of fire. The same fire had once protected the Aryan nomads from the bitter cold of icebound plains and snuffling predators outside dark caves. Now members of a dying strain these children of Aryan forebears were still its faithful guardians. The sun of the Fire worshippers had crossed the heavens and was on the decline. Nurturing it with enfeebled hands, a near-extinct race still walked around it; their journey's reach defined by its sacred flames.

Abba Mian had been used to say, 'Not only have we divided humans on the basis of religion, we have meted out the same treatment to books. *Hayat Faryad* and *Qashf-ul-Haqaiq* by Muslim historians, belong to Dawar Ali, and *Kabir Bani* and Rahul Sankaritya's *From the Volga to the Ganga* are Rai Shatab's property. We disparaged Kabir and failed to appreciate Sankaratiya; in the process we buried a great piece of literature in the graveyard of books,'

The neatly folded newspaper flew through the air and landed on the balcony. Admiring the paper boy's aim, Birjees bent down to pick it up. A whiff of frankincense caught at her senses reminding her of the fakirs of her own faith, a begging bowl in one hand and in the other, a metal censer containing the burning embers of a piece of coal and a smattering of incense, walking from shop to shop, extending the fragrant smoking vessel into each doorway as they passed, blessing alike those who gave and those who did not.

She opened the *Dawn* and saw Cowasjee's advertisement on the back page. All day she waited for the phone to ring. The evening brought Cowasjee and a copy of the *Jang* with the same prominently displayed advertisement.

Birjees' heart was heavy that night. Ashraf Chacha was one of those people who believed in reading each word, each news item in a paper. Nothing was allowed to escape his eye. Indeed Abba Mian had often teased him about this habit, saying: 'It is more likely for the recording angels to miss out some act of omission or commission in their register than for Ashraf Mian to miss out any bit of news in the paper.' Then how had he missed seeing such a prominently placed advertisement?

The next day passed in the same way. It was possible that Ashraf Chacha did not read these papers. But there were others too. He was not the only family member living in Karachi. Was she to believe that none of them read the papers? Had they, on giving up their country, given up reading the news as well? Abba's death had changed all relationships. The loss of a highly placed and influential father had cancelled all ties with the living daughter.

The third day drew to a close. Cowasjee came home. Sitting down to tea with two unknown people in a strange city, Birjees drank from the cup of bitterness and broke the bread of humiliation. The curtains in the open doorway billowed in the breeze. The sky darkened and sounds floated up from the lamp-lit street. The sounds were not unfamiliar it was just that she was a stranger among them.

The doorbell rang. In the five days that she had been here, hardly any one had called. Only a few old Parsi couples with faded faces and arthritic limbs with whom the Cowasjee's conversed in Gujrati.

Cowasjee folded the newspaper and went to answer the bell. She heard the door open and the sound of a loud unfamiliar guffaw assailed her ears.

'It is our theatre-walla,' said Mrs. Cowasjee drawing a deep breath. 'Now he will declaim, speak lines from plays, turn into a whole chorus. Cowasjee and he were at school together. His father was an important man but *he* caught the theatre bug. He wanted to act and sing and dance in films, flirt with all the pretty girls. His father was furious. He said his nose would be cut and threw him out of the house. He went to Bombay, he went to Calcutta, he went to Delhi—he even went to Rangoon. He became a famous actor, but now he is an old man.'

The door banged shut and Birjees stood up disconcerted. 'I'll clear the tea things,' she said and picking up the tray quickly left the lounge and went into the kitchen. She had barely time to fill the kettle and place it on the stove when Mrs. Cowasjee walked in.

'Arré Birjees, don't waste your time making tea for him. Come evening and he will touch nothing but liquor. Already he must have had a tipple before coming here. His hipflask goes with him everywhere. He's scared of Cowasjee so he won't ask for a glass, but every ten minutes he'll go to the bathroom for a swig and shout: "Bhabhi dear Bhabhi, its ages since I ate your salt,"' she mimicked, as she took out cashews and toasted almonds from sparkling glass jars.

'All theatre folk come to this pass. When they are famous they live on clouds and when they fall they land in the gutter. Now what else can you expect? The fortune he made found its way to the liquor shop and Baijee's pandan. Now he lives in a hovel of a room on Napier Road. Sometimes when the mood takes him, he comes here. When he's with us he makes us laugh and when he leaves we weep for him. Ahura Mazda protect us all!' she touched her earlobes in a gesture of atonement and began to place the bowls of dried fruit on the tray.

'Shall I go to my room?' Birjees asked.

'Arré Baba, now why will you do that? Are you thinking of gossiping with the Keeper of the Blue Skies and giving Him news of the share market? What a girl with an upside down mind you are! Now be sensible Birjees. You will come and sit with me and listen to his talk. Such men don't come one's way everyday.'

Birjees took the tray from her.

The old actor was sitting in the drawing room—the hero whose domain had stretched from Bombay to Burma. A skeleton of a man in a threadbare suit, with sunken cheeks and faded visage. A shell of a man, feeding on memories of past glories.

'When I was in Bombay … When I was in Calcutta … In this very Karachi when I acted in "Husn-e-Farang" … I had the lead part and that bloody son of a sweetmeat seller, Pandit Narayan Prashad Betab Dehlavi … he put on airs … faugh! … from stirring pots and beating sugar to New Alfred Company's cub writer … Strange are the ways of the Keeper of the Blue Skies! "Husn-e-Farang"! It was performed for the Royal Coronation and I was Chambez, Prince of Persia … but that Karachi has disappeared without a trace. The world of theatre has been destroyed. The bioscope has changed everything.' When speech was exhausted he turned his attention to the cashews and roasted almonds.

A cavalcade of chocolate heroes and charming heroines paraded through Time's drawing room, and it nibbled away at them making a meal of the once beautiful men and women.

Oppressed by his talk, Birjees excused herself and went out on the balcony. Sitting there in the old rocking chair her thoughts turned to Naju Chacha. I wonder where he is now? He had been turned out by Chhoti Ammi to wander from door to door, homeless and alone. He too had caught the acting bug, falling in love first with the bioscope and then with the idea of stardom in Bombay, returning only when failure, starvation and tuberculosis drove him back. He was Abba's cousin. Chacha Najm-ul-Huda whom they addressed as Naju Chacha and whom his sisters-in-law had called 'Naju dancer' and 'Naju the jester'. His elder brothers had refused to let him step into the house where his father had died of grief and his mother had lost her mind because of him.

He had come to Abba Mian for help. Unable to keep him in his ancestral home, he had given him a room in an outhouse on the estate. Here, in her more lucid moments his mother would come, bringing food hidden under her shawl, and singing old lullabies would feed it to him morsel by morsel. Naju Chacha would eat it and wipe away his tears on the sleeve of his shirt.

Whenever a new film was released in Patna, he put on clean clothes and went to Abba Mian and meekly asked for money to 'meet some urgent need'. Without a word Abba Mian would put his hand in his pocket and give him some money. He would take it quickly, clenching the notes in his fingers as if like homing pigeons they were in danger of taking wing in the blink of an eye.

Birjees sat in the old rocking chair and Naju Chacha's ghost floated around her. Abba Mian's trips away from Patna were red letter days for Naju Chacha for then the mood for jollification would come upon him. Drunk and making merry his voice would rise in rollicking song that crossed the boundaries of space to find its way to Chhoti Ammi's ears whose taunts and recriminations would rain on Birjees' head.

Performers, actors, itinerant entertainers, hundreds of thousands of groups and races, known and unknown, have acted and will continue to act out their parts on the world's variegated stage and then be heard of no more. Cowasjee and Mrs. Cowasjee and others of their kind, today members of a moribund race, how glorious had been their past. Kaikhusro, the Sasanian king, had whipped the ocean waves into submission and imprisoned the seas when they dared to destroy his ships. Yet, when Time turned its back on their race, the Arab hordes, eaters of locusts and drinkers of camel's milk, had swept upon them in a thunder of hooves and flashing steel. The sacred fire had been desecrated and their books had been burnt. Countless numbers were put to the sword and countless others warded off death by denying the religion of their fathers. Among the survivors were those who sought sanctuary on the shores of India. Then why, Pervaiz, you who were named after one of the kings of the Fire Worshippers, why did you and so many others like myself, why did we turn our backs on our own people to set out on the quest for another sanctuary?

Time had not turned its back on us. Why did we turn our faces away from time?

It was on a Sunday, at around eleven in the morning when Birjees was in the kitchen beating eggs in a white china bowl that the telephone bell rang and her heartbeat quickened. It had rung many times during the past few days but nobody had asked for her.

Cowasjee called out, the call was for her. Sky and earth swirled around her—'Pervaiz' said the sky as it swung past her—'Pervaiz' echoed the revolving earth. She walked into the lounge. Cowasjee handed her the receiver and left the room.

'Is that Birjees beta speaking?' asked a faint male voice.

The voice belonged to neither Pervaiz nor Ashraf Chacha.

'This is Hasnat Ahmad calling' came the voice, 'Hasnu of Sabzi Bagh.'

A flash of memory brought recognition. This was one of Abba Mian's distant connections. He had been among the first to migrate to Karachi.

'This is Birjees Hasnu Chacha. How are you and Chachi?' she tried to collect her thoughts.

Hasnu Chacha was a straw in this limitless sea of people and to one who is drowning even a straw spells safety.

'I saw your advertisement some days ago, but today when I mentioned it to your Chachi she was furious with me. I could not think of any reason why you would remember me.' Burdened by years of the indifference and neglect known only to those who dwell on the fringes of prosperity, the uncertainty in Hasnu Chacha's voice, bred by the acceptance of his own insignificance in the scheme of things, cut her to the quick and she responded indignantly, 'How can you talk so! Why would I not remember you?

What he failed to understand was the fact that with her Ashraf Chacha living in the same city what had been the need to advertise her presence. It took Birjees a long time to explain to him that he had moved house and she did not know his new address.

'I don't know where he lives. We come across each other at weddings and other such occasions. I'll bring this matter up with your Chachi. She's in touch with a lot of our relations. I'll get back to you once I have some news for you.' He rang off without waiting for her reply.

Hasnu Chacha called again after lunch. Her Zebun Chachi and he wanted to come and see her. She handed the receiver to Cowasjee who began to give detailed directions on how to get to the flat.

Around four o'clock in the evening, the doorbell rang and Birjees went to the door. Wrapped in a black burqa, tiny Zebunissa Chachi stood before her. Zebun Chachi: thin, sharp featured with kohl darkened eyes and betel red lips, her sallow skin glistening under the cheap cold cream applied for the occasion. Time had not dealt kindly with her and years of dealing with the world had hardened the already sharp face.

Without giving Birjees the opportunity to so much as glance at Hasnu Chacha, she shrieked like a kite, flung her arms round her and broke into voluble tears. Dazed, it took Birjees a few minutes to realise that this fit of grief was a formal gesture of mourning for Abba Mian's death.

Zebun Chachi bombarded her with questions but had no idea of Ashraf Chacha's whereabouts. Undaunted by her own ignorance she offered glib comfort: 'Beta, even God can be found if you look for him, so how can we fail to find Ashraf Bhaiya? But until we do find him, you must stay with us. After all we have to face your father on the Day of Judgment. Where is your luggage?'

Birjees' heart sank. She had never imagined that this would be the outcome of her advertisement. But perhaps under the circumstances, moving in with them was the only way left her of finding Ashraf Chacha, Pervaiz and Surriya.

'The luggage can follow later Chachi. Just give me a few minutes to pack a few things and ask Uncle and Aunty for permission to leave.'

Mr. and Mrs. Cowasjee were in the lounge. 'Uncle, Bano Aunty,' she said. These people are distant relatives but I believe that through them I'll be able to trace my uncle. They want me to go with them …'

'All right, but let me have their address before you go,' Cowasjee replied getting up.

When Birjees came out of her room with her bag she was met by Mrs. Cowasjee who had a red velvet bag in her hand.

'Birjees, your jewellery.'

'Bano Aunty, I can't carry it with me wherever I go. Please keep it for me. It will be safe with you.' She gave her a hug and kissed her on both cheeks before going and standing with bowed head before Cowasjee; for a brief moment she felt Abba Mian's hand touch her head in blessing.

There were faces in the swirls of mist there were voices too and glimpses of lost worlds. A voice that carried the greenery of lush jungles and the sparkle of leaping rivers found its way to her. Startled, she sat up. There was no mist. No faces. No voices. The sheet with which she had covered herself was wet with dew and the wan light of the setting moon filled the tiny courtyard.

On the bed next to her Shama turned in her sleep. Some members of the family were sleeping in the veranda, others were inside the house. Birjees went to the pitcher of water in the veranda, filled a cup, drank from it and came back to her bed.

When the train had left Patna city she had not dreamed that she would fail to find her destination even after the destination was reached.

She had left the Cowasjees in the hope that it would be easier to find her uncle from Hasnu Chacha's house. But she had been here for five days now and every time she brought up the question of Ashraf Chacha's whereabouts, Zebun Chachi would apply a corner of her dupatta to her eyes and reproach her for wanting to leave them: 'Arré beta, we are not so poor that you are a burden to us. Stay with us for a few days.'

Her mouth filled with the bitterness of bile. Because of Qamar Bhai's influence in the house the beards seemed to grow longer by the minute. Each phrase, each sentence was replete with innuendo and obliquity, at every turn a reminder of obligation. Hasnu Chacha was hardly a presence and in any case he left for work at daybreak. The younger son Iqbal was a student at the local government school but his real interests lay in eating and loafing around. Shama was the only one on whose spontaneous innocence Zebun Chachi with her wheeling and dealing ways had failed to cast a shadow. She had been removed from school after the eighth class and in the few days that Birjees had been there she had often come to her and softly pleaded with her to convince her mother to let her go back to school.

Her request made Birjees look at her with interest. Zebun Chachi kept her daughter busy in the kitchen most of the day and she noticed the soiled and crumpled clothes, the work roughened hands and the short soot-begrimed nails.

After breakfast that day, when Qamar Bhai had left for work and Shama had done with household chores, she addressed her aunt: 'I am taking Shama with me to the post office.'

'Now what in the world has put this strange idea into your head?' replied Zebun Chachi setting aside the dish in which she was sifting the rice.

'I haven't written to any one since I came here. I just thought I'd go and buy a few stamped envelopes.'

Zebun Chachi argued that Iqbal would get the envelopes when he returned from school but Birjees refused to listen. Shama quickly put on her burka and ignoring the message in her mother's eyes, left the house with her cousin.

Crossing the empty plot they came out on Jamshed Road. Separated from them by the stream of traffic large, prosperous houses lined the other side of the road. Their original owners had left for India and the present owners were those who had come from India to settle. The coloured panes of glass in their windows and skylights shone in the bright sunlight and reminded her of the doors and windows of the living room at home. Filtered through the multi-hued glass the light would fall on the snow-white sheet that covered the floor and flood its pristine white with colour. She often went to the living room for riaz and the lozenges of green, indigo and red light would move across the white sheet with the light of the sun as the room filled with the high and low notes of her voice. Sunlight and colour, high notes and low and a snow-white sheet.

Nirmala too had lived in just such a house. They had rehearsed for days at her house for the College Drama Festival. The living room, the snow-white floor covering and a host of girls playing different parts, taking on different personae would cross and re-cross the floor treading the indigo, yellow, turquoise and mauve sunlight under their feet. She had played the part of Chinta in 'Bilwamangal' and her voice had risen to the music of the song to Krishna the flute player, beloved of Dwar des and vanquisher of evil:

Wo Krishan pyara, woh
Wo bansi walla
Wo Dwar des ka dullara …

Pervaiz had come to all the performances at the festival and on the day that 'Bilwamangal' was staged, had sat in the front row; and when, in the third scene of the third act, she had raised her voice in song, rejecting the pomp and circumstance of palaces and the beds of silver and gold, asking only for love's fulfilment, he had done his best to make her laugh. He had teased her mercilessly after the performance: 'what was the need of all these high strikes on the stage? All you had to do was to make your wishes known to me, and I would have cast a kindly glance in your direction.'

Someone shook her by the shoulder, 'Are you sleep-walking, Birjees Baji?' Shama had lifted her veil and was staring at her curiously.

'No I'm not!' She laughed sheepishly. They had reached the post office.

The evening meal over, they sat chatting in the courtyard. On their way back from the post office, Shama had wanted to make a detour to show Birjees the school she had left so reluctantly, but she had refused, promising to go by that way and even meet her teachers, when they went out to post her letters. Shama was telling her about her days in school when they were joined by Hasnu Chacha and Zebun Chachi.

'Shama, go inside for a bit will you,' Zebun Chachi said sitting down on the bed. Looking distinctly uncomfortable, Shama got up and left.

'Is everything all right, Chachi?' Birjees asked. Her heart had begun to beat uncomfortably fast.

'Yes, yes, it is. The thing is that the two of us have been thinking of raising a certain matter with you for the past so many days. Today your uncle discussed it with an acquaintance, who advised against hedging the issue as losses could be incurred if too much time was wasted in mulling over matters.'

'I don't understand—what losses?' Birjees looked at her aunt and uncle in surprise.

'Tell me beta, have you brought your papers with you,' said Hasnu Chacha finally unlocking his tongue.

'What papers, Chacha?'

'Your property papers, what else!' Zebun Chachi intervened before Hasnu Chacha could get around to uttering a word.

'What property?'

'Your father's property.'

'But what have I to do with those papers?'

'Now that's a new one! If you don't, who does?'

'Your aunt has this bad habit of interrupting,' Hasnu Chacha attempted to bring the conversation back on track. 'Here everyone is making claims against the land and property they left behind. A friend of mine is a lawyer, and when I told him about you, he suggested that I should bring him your papers. It would take him only a few months to enable you to get property here against your claim.'

Veil after veil lifted from Birjees' eyes as understanding dawned. 'I have brought no property papers with me Chacha.' Her voice fell strangely on her ears as if it was coming from the bottom of a deep well.

'I don't believe it! You mean you came all this way swinging your arms and empty handed?' Zebun Chachi's tone was sharp.

'Let's get this straight Chachi. To begin with, when Abba Mian is no longer there, what value do his possessions have? Secondly, Nudrat, Bhaiya, Chhotti Ammi, they're all there and Abba Mian's property belongs to them. How can I lay a claim to what is in their use?'

'There's something wrong with your head, beta. Here the whole world is making all sorts of claims—I don't know what you're talking about.' Zebun Chachi's tone was definitely angry.

'Chachi, all I'm saying is that I have brought no papers with me. Nor do I intend to make any claim for property here. As soon as I find Ashraf Chacha and get my life in some order, I'll apply for a job in a college. I do not believe in living off the largesse of others.'

'But tell me this; by what tenet of the Quran or by which Hadith is it wrong for you to claim what belonged to your father and to his father before him?' By her lights, Zebun Chachi had clinched the argument.

'Whether there is such a tenet or not, Chachi, I don't know. All I'm saying is that it's useless to argue with me on this matter,' Birjees got up with a gesture of finality putting all further conversation at an end. 'I'm sleepy Chacha. Is there anything else that you want to discuss with me?'

'No beta, what is there left to say? Your father should've made a lawyer of you. Who can argue with you? We had a duty to perform and we have done so. The rest is up to you.' Zebun Chachi continued to mutter and grumble for a while.

That night when she lay down on her bed, Shama was still awake. She softly touched Birjees' hand and whispered, 'don't mind my parents. They speak without thinking.'

'Don't! This is no way to speak of your parents Shama,' she chided.

'You're right, but parents too must merit the respect that is owed them.'

'All right, now that's enough. We are bound to respect our parents but when it comes to leading our own lives, it is up to us to decide when to take their advice and when to go against their wishes.'

'It is when you say things like this that I stare at you in amazement. You speak just like a man. Even my Bhaijan doesn't talk like this. Girls like you are not formed out of empty air. We are shaped by the homes in which we grow up. When my home is so unlike yours, how can I dream of becoming like you?' she replied with a hint of sadness.

'You're very bright, Shama. All you need is a touch of courage. Just resume your studies somehow and then wait for the magical metamorphosis!'

'Metamorphosis?'

'Metamorphosis—transformation—a miracle. Does that make sense to your wondrous brain?'

'I like that word,' and she began to laugh irrepressibly.

'What is all this giggling in the middle of the night?' Chachi's voice made itself heard from the verandah.

'Hush! Chachi's armies are on the attack. Go to sleep now before Babar's cannonade decimates Ibrahim Lodhi's forces!' whispered Birjees and Shama pulled the sheet over her head.

'Enough of preening and primping Qamar Bhai, I want to talk to you about something.' Birjees called out to Qamar who was combing his hair in front of the tiny mirror that hung on the wall outside the bathroom door.

'Allah! Allah! that you should call upon this mote of dust, this nobody! Good fortune smiles on me early today!'

'Well put! A hyperbolic flight in the exact vein of Master Nisar,' Birjees teased.

'So you would liken me to a mere actor—a clown from the stage?' replied Qamar, miffed by the comparison.

'Come, come Qamar Bhai, what world do you live in? Actors are known as artists in this day and age—and there you go talking of clowns and jokers.'

'But of course—after all if you don't grant the status of artists to performers, who will? All Patna resounded with praise of your plays. You were known for your voice!'

'Seriously, Qamar Bhai, I want to talk about something important.'

'Right, we'll change the subject. Why did you call me— though I must take leave to tell you that Ammi is extremely angry with you—I must say, you are very the limit! Here we have slum dwellers pushing through false claims and acquiring palaces and there you go, walking away from your palaces and property without a backward glance.'

'Look Qamar Bhai, Chachi is another matter, but I don't expect you to broach this subject with me. What other people do or don't do is not my concern. It is for me to decide what I must or must not do according to my lights. Now don't get me off the track—I want you to do something for me, though if Chachi gets even a whiff of it, she will be furious.'

'That sounds promising. You want me to take you somewhere—to see a film or to Café Firdous for a kulfi?' His interest caught, Qamar looked at her hopefully and dragging up a chair, sat down beside her.

'Good heavens above! No! Do you take me for a little girl on the look out for outings and entertainment?'

'Then what would Miss Birjees Dawar Ali have this beggar do for her? Do you want me to pluck out the stars from the firmament for you? Is it the moon that you want me to place at your feet—or is it my life that you desire?' he declaimed, with his hand on his heart.

'Qamar Bhai, you must immediately give up reading romantic fiction, otherwise the time will come when, eyes shut and hand on heart, you will respond in the same vein when Chachi asks you to get groceries for her. You'll certainly get clobbered for your pains.'

'You have quite ruined my mood. All right then, what is it that you want?' Qamar did not take well to teasing.

'Just this—Shama is very bright and she is keen to continue with her studies. Please, somehow, get her back into school.'

'Help Father! Do you realise that if I so much as mention this to my mother she'll apply her slipper to my back and count 'one' after a hundred strokes!'

'Come off it Qamar Bhai. You call yourself a man and can't even take a stand for something that is right?'

'You're a crafty woman! You have challenged my honour as a man and left me with nothing to say. But I'll make you eat your words—this very day I'll don my shroud and court martyrdom. I'll raise this issue with my mother—but remember, it won't be easy to bring her around and may take days before she gives in.'

'Whether it takes days or whether it takes weeks, just do as I say and I shall be your creditor always.'

'Always? My dear, you'll go away and won't even remember that you once met a man whose name was Qamar,' he replied bleakly.

'How can you talk so? Do you think it's possible to forget one's relatives?'

'Only if the relationships are intimate and very dear— only then do we remember them. I am not lucky like Pervaiz for whose sake you have given up everything and come to seek in this barren, dust-laden wilderness.'

'Don't be a bore Qamar Bhai. Had Abba Mian lived, the question of my leaving home would not have arisen. Now stop making me sad by recalling those times.'

'All right, let's talk of something else.' Qamar sat there staring at the palms of his hands as if trying to decipher what was written there; turning towards the kitchen, called out: 'Hey Shama, what about some breakfast?'

On their way back from the post office that day, Shama took her to see her school. Once there Shama talked non-stop like a little parakeet till Birjees dragged her away: 'Come, let's go now. It's getting late and Chachi will be angry and I still have a phone call to make from the Irani Hotel.'

From the school they made their way to the Irani Hotel where a payment of four annas gave them access to the telephone. It had been many days since she had left the Cowasjees and she was missing them.

Drenched with sweat they arrived at the Irani Hotel to be exposed to the stares of the men who almost dislocated their necks to stare at them. Advancing to the counter Birjees asked the Irani, who most probably was the owner of the hotel, for the use of the phone. 'Certainly, bibi,' he replied, taking the telephone out of its black wooden box and sliding it towards her: 'place your four annas here and make your call.'

She paid up her four-anna bit and dialed Mrs. Cowasjee's number. Shama had lifted her veil and was looking around her curiously. This was the first time that she had set foot in a hotel. All she knew was that whenever Abba Mian had an important phone call to make, this was where he came.

Mrs. Cowasjee answered the phone on the fifth ring 'Arré, Birjees,' she screamed, 'where have you gone? It is so lonely without you. Cowasjee misses you too. Tell me, you are happy living with your relatives?'

'I'm all right. How are you? and Uncle and Manuchehr?'

'We're all well, but we do miss you. Now listen, tomorrow we are holding a Charity Bazaar and I'll come in the morning and get you—let your relatives know. I was planning to come and see you this evening, but since you have phoned me, I'm telling you now that we'll come for you tomorrow morning at around ten o'clock. Be ready.'

'I'll be waiting, but won't it be a nuisance for Uncle? He has to go to Court in the morning ...'

'Now don't you start wagging your tongue at me. How I pick you up is my headache.' The familiar scolding voice was strangely comforting.

'Are you going somewhere tomorrow?' Shama asked as they stepped out of the hotel.

'Yes, Shama, Mrs. Cowasjee is coming for me tomorrow. She wants me to go with her to some Charity Bazaar—why don't you come with us too? We'll be back by evening.'

'No, Birjees Baji, Ammi will never give me permission to go—and even if she were to do so, saving face for you, I have neither the clothes nor the social graces for such a gathering.'

'Come, don't be so sensitive. There's nothing wrong with the clothes you have.'

'But you told me that Mrs. Cowasjee is a Parsi—and these people are very modern. I'll be terribly out of place among them. These big houses that we are walking by, they're all owned by Parsis.'

'Really? I thought they belonged to Hindu families.'

'No, this entire area is known as the Parsi colony. If ever you come out in the evening you will see many fashionably dressed old ladies out for a walk.' Shama was talking as they went along. 'The houses that belonged to the Hindus are on the other side—our own people have moved into them now.'

It was during dinner that night that Qamar stunned his mother by broaching the matter of Shama's education. When all attempts at gentle persuasion failed to convince his mother, he firmly announced that whether she liked it or not, his mind was made up and in a day or two he would take Shama to school for readmission. Seeing that nothing would make him budge, Zebun Chachi arose in high dudgeon and calling down imprecations on his head, retired to her bed. Later that night when Shama came to her bed, she reached out and clasped Birjees' hand tightly in her own.

'I'll never forget what you've done for me,' she whispered, her voice deep with emotion.

'Don't be silly, I never once opened my lips. It's all Qamar Bhai's doing,' she whispered back.

'Bhaijan did it because you asked him to, otherwise he would never have risked Ammi's anger.'

'No, no, it is not like that Shama; Qamar Bhai is a sensible man. Times are changing and he can tell which way the wind is blowing.'

'Who're you fooling Birjees Baji—yourself or me? Bhaijan likes you very much—he is very impressed by you—what he does not understand perhaps is how different you are from the rest of us—that you are another creature altogether, not meant for the likes of him.'

'No, Shama. You don't know what you're talking about,' Birjees answered somewhat disconcerted.

'I know what I'm saying, Birjees Baji, I'm not making up things. It's true, it's not just Bhaijan that I'm talking about—I'm not sure if even Pervaiz is good enough for you. I saw him once at a wedding—he's impressive to look at, true, but then how far do looks alone go.' She sighed and was silent.

Heavy with the hot summer scent of madhumalti flowers, the night air fanned the sudden fire in her heart. How many times on summer nights as redolent with the madhumalti as these, had she not walked by the Ganga with Pervaiz, Nudrat, Bhaiya and Abba Mian. Ruffled by an occasional breeze, the moonlit waters had stretched limitlessly before them like an unbroken mirror.

'I miss you Pervaiz—do you miss me too?' she asked the ambient air and received no answer. She turned and lay on her back. Above her, far above her, hung the mist of stars; it seemed that sleep had hidden itself somewhere in those impenetrable depths.

Morning brought no change in Zebun Chachi's mood. Instead of making her way to the kitchen, as was her wont, she had got up, washed and returned to her bed.

'That's enough, Ammi. Please get up and see to the house. Mrs. Cowasjee will be here soon to pick up Birjees.' Qamar went and stood at his mother's pillow. Early that morning Birjees had told him that she would be spending the day with the Cowasjees.

'What do I care whether anyone comes or goes! When has anyone considered my wishes—can I stop anyone from doing what they want?'

'If you refuse to understand what I'm saying, that is your wish; but please get up and join us for breakfast—and if even this simple request is beyond your comprehension, then there are other means of making you understand. You know my temper—in a little while, not a thing will be left standing in this house.' Qamar's tone was uncompromising in the extreme.

Shocked, Birjees saw Zebun Chachi get up and make her grumbling way to the kitchen, calling down curses upon her fate as she went.

'This is very wrong Qamar Bhai! Is that the way to speak to your mother?'

'It's the only language she understands. It would've taken days had I tried to coax her out of her black mood.'

Zebun Chachi had breakfast with them and returned to her bed. Before leaving for work Qamar went up to Birjees: 'You'll be back in the evening won't you?'

'But of course!'

She was ready and waiting when the car horn sounded. Shama leapt up and opened the front door. 'The car's come,' she told Birjees peeping out.

'I'm going Chachi and will be back by evening.' Her aunt muttered something under her breath, shut the pandan with a bang and lay down flat on the bed.

Giving a little pat on Shama's shoulder, Birjees walked to the door. Manuchehr and Mrs. Cowasjee were waiting for her in the car.

'Won't you come in for a while?' she asked as a matter of courtesy.

'We're late as it is,' replied Mrs. Cowasjee, gesturing to her to get into the car. Already out of the car, Manuchehr was holding the door open for her. Enquiring after his well being, she got in. She looked back as the car began to move. Shama was still there, leaning against the green door of the house, watching them go. The car speeded up, Manuchehr changed gears and turned the corner and Shama was no longer visible to her eyes.

'Have you found your other relatives yet?' Mrs. Cowasjee asked, turning around to address her.

'No, not so far.'

'How very strange! Cowasjee worries about you a lot. He'll be joining us for lunch—you'll meet him at the Charity Bazaar.'

'I hope you won't mind Birjees, if I make a small detour on the way? I have some medicines that must be delivered urgently.' Manuchehr's tone was apologetic.

'Take as long as you like,' Birjees replied with a light-hearted laugh. 'What difference does it make?'

'Of course it makes a difference,' said Mrs. Cowasjee testily looking at her watch. 'We'll be late and miss the opening of the bazaar. Manuchehr's head is stuffed full with his patients and there is room for nothing else!'

'Mama is like a little kid—she has to be there for the opening ceremony,' Manuchehr teased.

The car wound its way through different streets and came to a stop in a narrow lane with a few houses interspersed with empty plots. A radio blared from one of them, but despite the noise the place had a desolate air.

The car had been parked a little further down the lane from the house where the medicines were to be delivered. Manuchehr walked back to the house and Birjees heard him knock at the door. The minutes ticked away as they waited for him to return and Mrs. Cowasjee began to get impatient. Looking to see where he was through the rear window she saw that he was talking to a young man in a striped pajama suit. The earth and sky swung round in a dizzying motion; she felt she was about to faint and clung to the seat with both hands to stop herself from falling.

Did hours pass or was it only a moment? Apprehensively, refusing to credit her own eyes, she twisted around and looked once again—she hadn't imagined it—it *was* Pervaiz.

Manuchehr retraced his steps and returned to the car and Pervaiz moved towards the door of the house—everything was happening in slow motion—the minutes turned into weeks and the weeks elongated, stretched out and became months. He would enter the door and she would lose him once more. She shook herself awake. Desperately she opened the car door and called to him.

He turned at the sound of his name. They stood facing each other. He was staring at her as if he couldn't believe his eyes.

'Birjees, you?' his voice came to her across eons of time.

Now, any minute, he will extend her a noisy welcome, grab her by the arm and drag her excitedly into the house. He will yell for Surriya, raise the roof beams with joy, fill the house with noise, talk a lot of nonsense—she took another step towards him.

'When did you come?' His measured tone stopped her in her tracks—uncertain—who was this man? So controlled. So detached. Surely this was not Pervaiz.

'You're the limit Pervaiz!' she erupted. 'You moved house and forgot to tell me. You even forgot to leave a forwarding address with the neighbours. I wrote, sent a telegram—searched for you people at the station—advertised in the papers—looked for you everywhere. But you had disappeared—as effectively as if you had applied magical collyrium in your eyes to make you invisible.' The words tumbled out in one breath.

Perhaps Pervaiz was still unable to believe his eyes. Perhaps he was still stunned by her sudden appearance—as if she had sprung out of the ground.

Mrs. Cowasjee called to her and he came out of his trance. A slight smile touched his lips. 'I still can't believe it's you. I'm still not sure that I'm not dreaming.'

'Birjees, who are you talking to? We're getting late.' Distinctly annoyed, Mrs. Cowasjee called out to her again.

She couldn't understand why Birjees had left the car to talk to Manuchehr's patient.

'Aunty, this is Pervaiz. My uncle's son—the one for whom we had placed an advertisement in the papers.

Hurriedly Mrs. Cowasjee got out of the car. 'But this is wonderful!' Her face lit up with joy. 'Incredible! You've found your uncle and his family—this calls for a celebration!'

She took another step forward.

'You were going somewhere with your friends—don't spoil your programme for my sake. In any case no one's at home—they're all out—and I'm about to leave for work. I'll come for you in the evening. Or perhaps Doctor Sahib can bring you here?' He was talking fast. 'I'll take the address of your house from Doctor Sahib.'

A weight settled on her heart. What had happened to Pervaiz? Why was he talking in this strange way? So what if they were all out? So what if he was going out to work— the walls of the house were not going with him! I could stay alone in the house—they would all return in the evening— one thought came chasing after the other ...

'It's all right Pervaiz. I'll bring her back in the evening.' Gently Manuchehr touched her shoulder: 'Come Birjees! Mummy's getting late.'

She looked at Pervaiz in disbelief and he came swiftly up to her: 'Don't look so bewildered and upset. Go with Doctor Sahib. When you come in the evening we'll all sit together like old times and listen to the tale of your adventures and how you suddenly appeared from nowhere. Honestly, you are the limit—not even letting us know that you were coming. I've an appointment to keep—otherwise I would never send you away like this. As it is, I have to get dressed and will leave as soon as you go. What will you do alone in the house? You can't spend the day talking to the walls! ThisYes house doesn't even contain a sitar; otherwise you could've kept yourself busy twanging away at it.'

The reeling world steadied and came to a stop. Yes this was the old Pervaiz with his nonsensical talk and the mocking, mischievous smile that she loved so much.

'Come, come, don't just stand there—get a move on,' he said pushing her towards the car and shutting the door after her. He bent down to peep at her through the window. 'There now, don't look so woebegone. Go smiling—this evening it will be like old times. Surriya misses you so much.'

Manuchehr started the car and she felt like asking, 'and how much have *you* missed me?' But she could ask nothing, say nothing to him. Pervaiz raised his hand in farewell and the car picked up speed. Soon he was lost to sight and they were bowling down the main road.

Leaning back against the seat she heaved a deep sigh and closed her eyes. The hum of traffic receded and her thoughts moved to Zebun Chachi. She would be prostrated by this news. Leave alone trying to find Pervaiz and the family, she had not let even a mention of their names escape her lips.

Mrs. Cowasjee's voice cut across her thoughts jerking her back to the present, 'Now all your worries are over Birjees. I hope you'll invite us to your wedding!'

'There is no gainsaying Mummy's logic! Where did the idea of Birjees' wedding spring from?' Manuchehr queried.

'My dear, she's found her fiancé. Of course she'll get married. What else do you expect her to do—sell dumplings?'

'What fiancé?'

'Arré Baba, that boy—the one you were gabbling away to!

'Is Pervaiz really your fiancé? Or is this one of Mummy's fantasies?' Manuchehr asked, turning briefly to look at her.

Her face red to the roots of her hair, she took shelter in prevarications. 'Pervaiz is my cousin. It is his family that I came to stay with in Pakistan.'

'I see,' he said in a low voice. His foot went down on the accelerator and the car flew with the wind.

By the time they reached Beach Luxury Hotel the Charity Bazaar was in full swing. Despite the tangled confusion of her thoughts she was distracted by the variety of stalls and the colourful display of objects for sale. Snow-white organdy, exquisitely embroidered in pastel silks depicted a whole world of flowers and leaves in shades of pink, pale yellow, blue, green and crimson lake. Saris, children's dresses, napkins, tablecloths—they were there to gladden the eye along with mirror encrusted handbags, hand painted pottery, handmade dolls, stuffed teddy bears, bunny rabbits and much else besides.

They hadn't been there long when Cowasjee joined them. Mrs. Cowasjee greeted his entry with a shriek and talking at the speed of what seemed like a hundred and fifty words a minute, poured out the tale of the day's happenings to him. 'So much for all your worrying and fretting,' she concluded, 'didn't I tell you things would sort themselves out—but did you listen to me? No!'

'All right, now just be quiet for a bit,' Cowasjee replied dampeningly.

'I? Why should I be quiet?' Mrs. Cowasjee replied pugnaciously, ready to take him on.

'OK Mummy, relax. Let's have some lunch first,' Manuchehr intervened, and despite his mother's, 'Wait a bit and stop knocking foreheads with me,' shepherded them into the dining room.

The hotel was on the beach and there was the sun-dazzled sea and a tang of saltwater and seaweed in the air. Lunch, and after lunch, Cowasjee's flat. She was in thrall to slow moving, somnambulant Time. Would evening never come? She longed to look again at Pervaiz, meet Surriya—Karachi had wrought a strange change in Pervaiz—made him unfamiliar—or perhaps it was just the effect of shock—of seeing her so unexpectedly.

Silent, lost in his thoughts, Manuchehr joined them for tea. She wanted to ask him about Pervaiz. How had they met? How well did he know him? The ease with which Pervaiz had suggested that he should drop her off at their house suggested a modicum of familiarity. Questions arose unbidden to her lips but remained unasked.

'I'll go fetch your jewellery. You better pack your things Birjees,' Mrs. Cowasjee arose from the chair as she spoke.

'Come, Mummy, what's the hurry? Let Birjees take a few things—her suitcase and jewellery can follow later—I'll drop them off myself once she settles in. And yes, Birjees, before going to Pervaiz' house, we must stop by at Jamshed Road to inform your relatives of the change in your circumstances.'

Mollified, she looked at Manuchehr. To her shame she realised that the one brief meeting with Pervaiz had driven all thought of Shama and Zebun Chachi from her mind—it was as if they had never been.

'Now isn't that nice Birjees, my dumb son has spoken,' Mrs. Cowasjee laughed, teasing Manuchehr about his habitual silence.

'I speak when there is something worth saying Mummy. What can I do if you think I'm dumb?'

'Yes, yes, only you and your father have things worth saying. I'm the empty vessel—a lot of noise and no sense!' Mrs. Cowasjee replied, peeved by her son's response.

And then they were out of the house and in the blink of an eye had reached Zebun Chachi's house. Shama was at the door as the car drew up—she must have been waiting for them at the window; that was why was at the door so quickly.

She got out of the car and Shama came up to her, 'You're very late Bajiya—my eyes have turned to stone waiting for you. Ammi has been asking after you too—Qamar Bhai was just going out to phone and check if everything was all right,' Shama complained, her affectionate tone belying the criticism in her words.

'You're a fine one, beta! To stay out so late in a strange city—what if you had lost your way or come to some harm? How would your Chacha have faced your father's spirit?'

'For God's sake Amma, you do talk without thinking. Birjees was with friends—they are responsible people, no harm could have come to her while she was with them and in any case what has all this to do with her father's spirit?' Qamar cut short his mother's complaint and turned towards her, 'but why are you standing there as if ready to take off with the wind? Why don't you sit down?'

'I have something to tell you Qamar Bhai.'

'Is everything all right?'

'Yes, it's just that I've found Ashraf Chacha.'

The words were hardly out of her mouth, when Zebun Chachi, who had been lying on her bed, sat bolt upright. 'What? What did you say?' Her voice was sharp with displeasure. 'You have found Ashraf Bhai?'

'Yes, Chachi—it was quite by chance that I found his house—I have still to meet Ashraf Chacha, but I ran into Pervaiz this morning.

'So, you've met Pervaiz?' Qamar asked dryly.

'Yes, we've met, and I've come to tell you, that I shall be moving in with them.'

'But of course beta, you have found your real relatives and you must go to them. After all, what claim do we have on you? We belong neither with the few nor with the many—what relevance do we have? Ours was just a knot in a cotton thread.' Chachi lashed out venomously.

'Ammi, for God's sake, don't say anything more!' Shama begged tearfully then turned towards Birjees and asked, 'Baji, will you leave us now?'

'I'll stay with both families. Just because I've found Ashraf Chacha doesn't mean that our relationship is at an end.'

The horn sounded impatiently cutting them short. 'Shama, I must get my things—they're waiting for me,' she hurried out of the room.

'Pervaiz is to be envied. Truly fortune smiles on him. There is much to be said for those who say that like calls to like. People get lost in fairs and you ended up finding Pervaiz.'

Making no attempt to reply, she began to fold her clothes and stuff them into her bag. Hasnu Chacha was out and Zebun Chachi's angry mood made leave taking less difficult. The difficulty lay with the weeping Shama. Birjees kissed her tear-wet cheeks and quickly left the room. It wasn't easy.

The distance to Pervaiz' house was traversed in silence and her heart beat fast as they turned into his street. Manuchehr sounded the horn and the car slowed to a halt. She had barely stepped out when the front door opened and Surriya rushed out and folded her in her arms. Surriya!

Her own blood. Home. Safety. Pervaiz. She held back her tears with some difficulty.

'Wouldn't it be better if this very affecting scene were to be enacted indoors?' Pervaiz' voice and then Pervaiz himself in a snow white kurta pajama. There was light everywhere.

She laughed and pulled herself together. Remembering the ones seated in the car, she turned towards them. Mr. and Mrs. Cowasjee's faces reflected pleasure and contentment, but Manuchehr was staring at her, a strange expression on his face. Catching her eye, he lowered his gaze.

Despite Surriya's and Pervaiz' insistence, the Cowasjees' refused to stay. 'We'll come another time,' they said. Cowasjee place a protective hand on her head in farewell and Mrs. Cowasjee kissed her on both cheeks before getting into the car, then the good people whose presence, like kindly moonlight, had lightened the dark night's shadows, drove away.

The house was built on a high plinth and a few steps led up to a deep and spacious verandah. The front door was open and following Pervaiz into the house she was reminded of the tiny baithak of her cousins' house in Patna, furnished solely with a takht and its complement of a spread and two bolster pillows.

'Now just sit down and relax. Ammi and Abba are out. There was some kind of a function at the house of one of Abba's senior officers and much as they would have liked to be here for you, they couldn't get out of that engagement.

'Has Ashraf Chacha got himself a job then?'

'He's the purchase officer in a government department.'

'I'm afraid none of this is making very much sense to me.'

'There is much that won't make sense to you,' Surriya murmured in a low voice.

'Why are you sitting here and jabbering away? What about getting us something to drink?' Pervaiz looked warningly at his sister and she got up and went inside.

Silence settled in the space vacated by Surriya. She waited expectantly for Pervaiz to speak; say something to her, but he sat there without uttering a word as if he had forgotten how to talk. Apprehension tugged at her senses and she swivelled around to face him. Discomfited by her gaze he burst into speech.

'You should have written to me about your coming— and this Dr. Manuchehr and his family—since when have you known them?'

'You're a fine one to say that! First you left for Pakistan without informing me. Then you hardly wrote to me, and on top of it all, when you changed houses you failed to give me your new address. Why would I not write and inform you about my decision to come here? You had moved house and both my letter and the telegram missed you. When I found neither you nor Ashraf Chacha at the station, I made my way straight to your P.I.B house only to find …'

'That the physician had shut shop and gone elsewhere,' cut in Surriya as she entered with a tray bearing glasses of orange squash. Ice cubes tinkled against the misty sides of the imported French tumblers.

'You have to add your little morsel don't you. You can't seem to shed the habit—just try saying nothing for a change. ' Once again Pervaiz glared warningly at his sister—'yes, what happened then?'

'It's a long story Pervaiz, if I tell it to you now, I'll have to repeat it all over again for Chacha and Chachi, and I can't bear to do that. Let them come home and then I'll tell you all about it in one go,' she replied taking the glass that Pervaiz held out to her.

'Good idea. But tell me, how was every one at home? How are Chhotti Chachi, and Nudrat and Bhaiya? They must have been upset at your leaving?

'Chhotti Ammi, Nudrat, Bhaiya—they were all well when I left them; but they are no longer in Patna. The Bhanwar Pokhar house has been sold.'

'Good heavens! The house sold?' Surriya choked on her drink.

'Yes, it's been sold. Chhotti Ammi always had a thing against it.' For a moment the shadow of the house fell across her heart.

'That was not well done. I find it hard to believe—had she no compunctions about selling the house that Chachajan had built with so much care?' He asked disbelievingly.

'And why are you so surprised? Here you are all of you, making claims for houses and shops in lieu of the homes you left behind, and that's all right. But if Chhotti Chachi, who has remained where she belongs, has sold her own house, that becomes a matter of concern and condemnation. She only sold a house made of bricks and mortar; here people are selling their very souls for gain and nothing seems to affect their comfort.' The underlying sharpness in Surriya's voice made Birjees sit up and look sharply at her. Where had this bitterness come from? What was the cause of this poisoned speech?

Birjees looked on silently and the melting ice cubes tinkled against the thin transparent sides of her glass.

'Since when have you learnt to dawdle over your sherbet? Why don't you drink it up and be done with it. In a little while Abba and Ammi will arrive and then who knows how long it will take you to narrate the saga of all your woes. Come to think of it, Surriya, make sure you serve dinner first—it will be dawn before we sit down to eat if Birjees gets in first with her Amir Hamza dastaan. I'll die of hunger if that happens.'

'How very ungracious of you Pervaiz,' she said dryly, taking a sip from her glass. 'Am I to understand that you are not even willing to listen to my story?'

'Listening to you talk one would think you had walked all the way from Patna, and arrived this minute, clad in a shuttlecock burka, dragging your feet across a thousand miles of India, when in actual fact you came here this morning in Dr. Manuchehr's fancy car and even now it was his limousine that drove up to this humble door for you to step out daintily and enter the house!' His tone belied the dryness of his words and the momentary tension was released.

'Birjees, you talk to Bhaiya while I take a peep in the kitchen,' Surriya interrupted leaving the room.

'There's a lot of activity today in the kitchen, and the menu presents quite a change from our daily diet of lentils, courgettes and bitter gourd. I believe there is a chicken simmering in the pot, not to mention the pulao and shahi tukray. Your arrival has wrought a full scale revolution in the kitchen!'

'And why does it bother you if Chachi and Surriya choose to pamper me?' she replied getting up.

'Now where are you off to?' he asked

'To lend a hand in the kitchen. God knows how much time Surriya's spent there in this heat.'

'Now don't you go wasting your sympathy on her. She's not the oppressed maiden you think her to be. She hasn't gone into the kitchen to put herself through any hardship— it's the cook who has to put up with her pestering.'

'Oh, but that's wonderful. I'm so glad you've got a cook. It must have taken a lot of load off Chachi and Surriya.'

'That it has, and Ammi especially spends her day reclining on her bed.'

'You'll get a piece of Chachi's mind if she hears you say that about her,' she replied laughing at his nonsense.

'Oh but I only say such things when I know that Ammi is at least a mile's distance away from the house.'

'Enough of that, tell me about yourself. What are you doing now? Have you not got a job yet?—I'm asking because you were still at home at 11 'o clock this morning,' she turned and paused interrogatively at the door.

'I've started my own business.'

'Your own business? And what exactly does that mean? Judging by the level of comfort and ease in the house, you must be doing very well. Your letters gave me to understand that you were still looking for a job and not too successfully at that. You sounded quite worried—there was never any mention of your setting up a business of your own?'

'That's an old story. I did look for a job for a few months after coming here. Then I was introduced to a man who owns a large and successful business concern. He needed someone responsible to manage his affairs for him. When he met me—

'He straightway fell for you hook, line and sinker— isn't that so Bhaiya? Isn't that what you were going to say?' Surriya had come in, and catching her brother's last sentence, jumped midstream into the conversation.

'I was coming to help you in the kitchen and just stopped to ask Pervaiz something.'

'There's nothing for you to do there. Everything's ready, I just went for a final look. Dinner will be served the moment Abba and Ammi return. Now, don't just stand there, come and sit,' putting her arm around her waist Surriya drew her to the sofa beside her.

'Ah yes, you were telling me about this man who saw you and, to use Surriya's words, fell for you hook, line and sinker?'

'Absolutely! After all am I not the boy who was born with a star on his forehead and the moon on his chin?'

'All right, all right! So now you have entered the pages of the dastaan. Stop confusing yourself with the princes who dwell there—we know you for exactly what you are. What I want to know is what happened after this man fell so madly in love with you?

'What could have happened?' Surriya interrupted not giving her brother a chance to speak. 'He met the same fate as all those princes who set out on a quest for Gauhar Murad and end up falling foul of the jinn and become his prisoners. Bhaiya too has been captured by an ogre who has turned him into a parrot and put him in his pocket for safety.'

'I seem to get the feeling that Surriya has some grievance against you,' said Birjees looking intently at her cousin.

'The grievance is simply this, she wants her beloved brother, who is the apple of her eye and for whom she is willing to sacrifice her every wish, to spend all his time with her, and this is precisely what the pressures of work in a successful and growing concern won't allow! I'm out most of the day—and often for two or three days at a time. This luxurious way of life does not come for free—it exacts a price,' he replied with barely concealed irritation.

'I know nothing comes for free. All I'm saying is that one should take stock of the situation to ensure that not too high a price is being paid for what one is getting,' Surriya muttered softly under her breath.

Sensing that the brother and sister were on the brink of a full-fledged quarrel she caught Surriya's hand and drew her out of the living room saying, 'come let's go and take a peep in the kitchen.'

There, Birjees was greeted by a most competent looking cook. 'He is from Purab and believes in interlarding his speech with swear words, especially with reference to himself. Despite all her efforts Ammi hasn't been able to rid him of the habit.' Surriya informed her in a low aside before presenting him to her, 'This is Sadiq, Birjees, and on his own evaluation, the master of his craft.'

'Arré Bibi, the days when I could call myself master of anything are gone forever. I was a master cook when I lived in our part of the world but not any more! Not here where I can buy neither spices nor herbs. Good cuisine requires flavour and flavour is not something that resides in this God forsaken Sadiq's ladle, to be conjured up by the stirring of the pot. Neither nutmeg nor mace can I find here. Go to the hakim's they tell me at the pansari's. And why should I do that, I ask. It's not a medical prescription that I'm seeking!' Sadiq rattled on as he removed a biri from behind his ear and tapped it on the matchbox.

'Well, Sadiq, today I'll eat food cooked by you, but from tomorrow I'll take charge of the kitchen. I'll give you my recipes and teach you a whole range of new dishes—but before I do that, you'll have to pass my test.' Birjees lifted the lid from one of the pots and examined the food as she spoke.

'What test?' asked Sadiq in surprise.

'The test in which I'll look at your recipes for karhi, shabdeg and Bihari kebabs.'

Someone knocked at the front door. 'That must be Abba and Ammi. Answer the door, Sadiq; and Birjees, quickly, please come away otherwise I'll be scolded for exposing you to the smoke and heat of the kitchen.'

Pervaiz had beaten Sadiq to the door and Chacha and Chachi had entered the house.

Her heart contracted with pain when she saw Ashraf Chacha—how like Abba Mian he was. Unable to control the rush of tears, she ran into his arms.

After dinner that night, in the dim half-light of the courtyard, seated amidst those linked most nearly to her by the bonds of blood, she allowed the demons and back-footed ghouls of those friendless days and nights to come out into the open. And thus was unfolded the tale of her long journey—a journey marked by the betrayals and severities of loved ones and the kindness of strangers. It was a tale more strange than any to be found in the *Talism-e-Hoshruba*, for the protagonists of this dastaan were the shifting sands of a once safe and familiar geography made unfamiliar by the legerdemain of history and bewitched and held in thrall by time.

It was drawing close to morning when she lay down on her bed next to Surriya and realised that at last she was among her own people. The blue bulb cast a faint light in the room and above her the ceiling fan whirred endlessly. Pervaiz was in the adjacent room. He had asked her no questions! Said nothing to her! But then, why should he have done so? There was no need—speech after all was a medium of exchange between strangers, not friends.

'I have so much to say to you Birjees.' Surriya raised herself on her elbow and looked at her. 'Even now I shudder to think of what could have happened to you on that dark night when you took Mrs. Cowasjee's brooch to her. What if they had been the wrong kind of people? What if she hadn't dropped the brooch—or if you hadn't found it?'

'I don't know—I have begun to feel that 'if' is the most significant word in my life. Just think about it—if Abba Mian had not been in such a hurry to leave us—if you people had not left the country in such haste—if you hadn't moved house or if you had left a forwarding address!' There was deep sadness in her voice as she uttered these words.

'I did write to you—in great detail,' Surriya answered softly, 'the letter probably got there after you'd left Patna. I wonder in whose hands it fell.'

'The postman must have torn it up and thrown it away. Everyone knew I had left the country.'

'What difference does it make whether anyone read it or tore it to shreds and threw it away? The fact is that there have been a lot of 'ifs' in your life. I'm still mystified by the advertisements. How could we have missed them?' Surriya sounded puzzled.

'Pervaiz did say that there was one day when the paper wasn't delivered,' Birjees reminded her. 'In any case so much has happened to me that nothing surprises me anymore.'

'You're right,' said Surriya and sighed deeply.

At breakfast next morning Birjees was startled to find that Pervaiz had already left for work. His absence continued to bother her throughout the meal. Strange that business affairs should take precedence over human relations. I have come so far and after such an arduous and frightening journey, and he couldn't take even a day's leave from work—or if that were not possible, surely he could've waited long enough to have breakfast with me. After all, yesterday he had been in no hurry to leave for work.

As soon as breakfast was over Chachi went to her room. Surriya, too, seemed preoccupied—at first she kept riffling through the morning paper, then left the room saying that she had something to say to Sadiq.

Fleetingly it entered her mind that Surriya was avoiding her. Accusing herself of paranoia she dismissed the thought.

Feeling a little lost, she wondered what to do with her time, then remembered that Chacha Roshan Rai had asked her to write to him on reaching her family. She had given him her power of attorney for the sale of the fruit orchards. Perhaps they had been sold by now—she should write to him; give him Ashraf Chacha's address so that he could remit the money to her.

'Surriya, could I have an aerogramme?'

'I've run out of them. Maybe Bhaiya has some.'

'Could you get one for me? There's a letter I must write; if I do it now Sadiq can mail it when he goes to the bazaar.'

'I've nothing to do with Bhaiya's things. I don't even set foot in his room. Why don't you get it yourself; the stationery is sure to be in the writing table drawer.'

Surprise held her in check for a moment. What was going on in this house? The two had always been close to each other; ever since she could remember, Pervaiz had been the adored brother.

The proportions of Pervaiz's room and the elegant furniture came as a pleasant surprise. She walked up to the writing table and pulled open the top-most drawer, only to find that it held nothing more than a few bills and letters. Pushing it shut, she tried to open the next drawer but it stuck after sliding out for a few inches. Catching sight of a writing pad in the aperture, she gave it a tug. It slid forward another inch but still held fast. Sliding her hand into the open space she tried to pull out the piece of paper that was jamming it.

What a careless man he was to be sure; stuffing everything pell-mell into the drawer. She yanked at the obdurate piece of paper and drew out a folded newspaper—at the same time the drawer slid open. Letter pad and envelopes were there for the asking, but Birjees' eyes were fixed on the folded paper in her hand.

A dark chasm opened beneath her feet. Unconsciously she held on to some object to save herself from falling into the fiery, serpent infested depths of hell as the writhing reptiles and demons clamoured to pull her in. It couldn't be true—she was in the middle of a nightmare—she must wake up. What was that film she had once seen in Lucknow with the sterile ice-cold morgue and the rows of dead bodies, each one lying motionless in its appointed shelf, waiting to be claimed—and before her the stinking corpse of the few day's old newspaper—waiting patiently to be claimed. Its discovery signified the end of the search, and with it, the end of the story. The search was over. It was the end of the quest.

'Where have you got to? You seem to be glued to that room.' Surriya entered and then stopped short on seeing Birjees. She moved forward and took the paper from her hand. 'But this is an old ...' the sentence remained incomplete—'where did you find this?' she asked horror-stricken.

Birjees pointed towards the drawer. Carrying the corpse of the long dead paper Surriya walked out of the room. She could hear her own voice talking, crying deliriously but could make no sense of the words. 'Hush!' she wanted to say, 'Hush! There has been a death in the house, don't make so much noise.'

She was sitting on the cold stone floor. Surriya came in and caught her by the hand and took her into her own room. 'Why don't you cry? Catch them by their robes and confront them with their treachery?' Surriya shook her savagely then collapsed in a storm of tears.

When the stable earth is dragged away from beneath one's feet and the sheltering sky is yanked aside, there is no room for tears. The eyes, like disused, waterless wells, have no moisture to shed.

'That is why I wrote to you—asking you to make haste—before matters got out of hand.'

Birjees raised her eyes and looked at her—Pervaiz' engagement had taken place a month earlier. The chosen bride was Jamshed sahib's daughter; her dowry included half ownership of the business for the groom. Bhaiya was to be a rich man—that is why they had left the old lodgings and moved to this big house. ... 'I wrote and told you all about it in my last letter.' Surriya's words fell on her ears like counterfeit coins in a beggar's bowl; all ties, all relationships all rituals were annulled, empty—Ashraf Chacha, who was Abba Mian's own blood—Chachi, who was her mother's cousin and her closest friend—the silver on the clay shard—and on the other side—the false claims for property and Pervaiz' prospective father-in-law with extensive business interests and the transformative, magical power of money. It was the hour of the dastaan; of Jamshed in a world where everything was up for sale—every bond without meaning, each relationship weighed against gold. The new Moses had accepted exile from the land of his birth so that he could barter himself for gain.

Words were mere noise. She blocked her ears against them. 'Surriya, I want to hear nothing; know nothing.' Sunlight climbed down from the window and set the bed on flames and the rest was oblivion.

The sun had set and it was evening. A light rain began to fall—*chaltay ho to chaman ko chaliyé, kehtay hain ke baharan hai—phool khillay hain paath harray hain, kam kam baad o baara hai ... let us go, if you will, to the garden for spring is here—flowers blossom, the walks are green; a small rain falls and there is a breeze ... challi simt-i- ghaib se ik hawa keh chaman zahoor ka jal gia ... a wind arose from an unknown quarter and the glory of the garden was destroyed ... main paapan kuchh aissi jalli na koela bhai na raakh ...*

fire—ashes—I, a sinner burnt in such a flame that I became neither coal nor ash …na tau mein raha na tu tu raha, jo rahi so bekhabri rahi, kitab aqal ki taaq par joon dhari thi toon dhari rahi … for I was no longer I and you were transformed; what remained was a forgetting an understanding beyond desire, beyond the knowable—unheeded, forgotten on the shelf lay the book of reason. (Mir Taqi Mir)

She is sitting in the veranda. Her body feels scorched. Ashraf Chacha has come home from work and on finding that she has discovered the truth has gone silently to his room. Surriya walks about restlessly like a soul in torment. The sky is full of birds, homeward-bound. She stares at them fixedly. Surriya come and sits besides her, waiting for her to speak, to say something.

A car stopped outside the house; a door banged shut. Birjees tensed. Pervaiz had come home. Sadiq opened the door before Pervaiz could ring the bell. A few minutes later he entered the house laden with a host of paper bags and baskets and took them into the kitchen. Pervaiz came in shutting the door behind him. His eyes fell on Birjees and he came towards her. On seeing him Surriya vacated the chair.

'Hey! Where are you off to? I'll get another chair for myself.' Without a word Surriya went into her room.

Pervaiz sat down and stretched his legs before him. Birjees looked at him in the oblique evening light. How well she knew that face. It had been part of her childhood and each feature, each expression was imprinted indelibly in her mind. One glance from him had the power to quicken her blood. Today that face belonged to a stranger, alien and unfamiliar.

'Well Birjees, and how have you entertained yourself today?' He bent down to untie his shoe laces before slipping them off. Pulling off his socks he tucked them into the shoes and placed his bare feet on the cool stone floor.

'I entertained myself according to the plans you laid out for me,' she replied forcing a smile.

'You gave me no chance to plan, arriving unannounced out of the blue as you did. You caught us unawares; there was no time to prepare a fitting welcome for you. I've got some fruit and other things for you.'

'So now you buy a welcome from the bazaar for those who come to your house?'

Alerted by her dry tone he laughed ruefully. 'You have a point. There was a time we couldn't have imagined buying anything other than fruit, vegetables and spices from the bazaar, but the thing is that Surriya has become lazy and refuses to go into the kitchen.' He was silent for a while, then said, 'Birjees, I have to go out of Karachi for a couple of weeks, so I've taken tomorrow off to take you around a bit. We'll go to the beach. I've made arrangements for a car and a beach-hut.'

Birjees stared at him in disbelief. Was this Pervaiz or some consummate actor skilfully delivering his lines?

'Sadiq! Sadiq!' turning aside he yelled at the kitchen door and Sadiq leapt out in answer to the summons: 'Yes, Bhaiya?'

'What is all this "yes Bhaiya!" Are you planning to give me my tea or not?'

'It's brewed; it'll be here in an instant.'

'Why so silent? Tell me your gossip and listen to some of mine. What do you plan to do now that you are here? What new bee in your bonnet have you got?' He asked laughingly. Before she could think of a reply, Chachi called out to him. 'Coming Mother,' he replied like a dutiful son and made to get up.

'Stay a moment Pervaiz. It's better that I tell you what you are bound to hear from Chachi.'

The seriousness of her tone made him pause, 'I'll be with you in a minute Mother,' he called out, then turned and looked enquiringly at her. 'Is everything all right? What is it that you want to tell me?'

'Nothing of any importance really. At least it's nothing that you don't already know. I just wanted to tell you that I've found the newspaper—the one carrying the advertisement of my arrival in Karachi.' Her voice was keen like a knife.

For a second he seemed to lose colour. 'Where did you find it?' he asked pulling himself together.

'In the drawer of your writing table.'

'And who gave you the right to riffle through my things?' Instead of being embarrassed Pervaiz mounted a counter attack.

Something snapped inside her and the tamped down fire flared up. 'Following Surriya's advice, I went looking for an aerogramme. In other words, I looked for enlightenment, but coming face to face with the Truth, found prophet-hood instead.'

'Well, all right. In a way I'm glad you've found out everything by yourself. It makes my task easier. The fact is Birjees, our engagement was based on a whim of our elders and it has ended with them. You are an extremely headstrong person, and once you set your mind on something, you have to achieve it no matter the cost. I don't like such women.

'You decided to go to Lucknow for your MA and neither Chacha Jan nor I could make you change your mind. Before that, you got it into your head to learn music, and not only did you take singing lessons, you learnt to do it professionally and your programme was broadcast on radio.

'We came to a parting of ways. I came here because I saw a future before me in this country. Had I stayed on, I would have frittered away my life at some petty clerical job. I could not even imagine that you would come here. Had I even a whiff of a suspicion about your plans, I would have written and told you everything.'

With what ease and seeming transparency did he tell his tale.

'You saw the advertisement and you hid it—not from the entire family, but from Surriya. Chachi's and Ashraf Chacha's silence speaks their guilt—did Ashraf Chacha not remember his dead brother? I am your cousin, your uncle's daughter—your own blood! Is it customary to cut connection midstream? Or is white the colour of all migrant blood?' She was in the eye of the storm; gales, earthquakes buffeted and shook her world. Her whole body was on fire.

'The advertisement was addressed to all your relatives—it did not specifically name either Abba Mian or myself. There are others here besides us.'

She tried to recognize the speaker—but he had travelled light years away from her and she could not make out his features.

Everything had turned to ashes—relationships, affinities, love, affections, norms, customs, little acts of kindness. This man who sat before her—what was he to her? She tried to remember—this man whose features resembled those of her dead father, and who now refused to meet her eyes, what did she have to do with him? Abba Mian's features were not unique—there were many others who looked like him. Was it nothing then, to be born in the same family; be part of a shared culture, owning a way of life, a particular history?

Flames engulfed her body, her mind, her sensibilities—she got up and the world swung around her; she clung to the chair for support. Someone was holding her; there were voices—

'she has fever, her body is burning'—

'wait, let me call the doctor'—

Whose voice was that?

'Abba Mian? I want Abba Mian!'

'Birjees! Birjees!' someone shook her.

Surriya's face swam before her—she shut her eyes. She tried to get up.

'I want to go home—to Abba Mian.' Everything had turned red—Surriya; the walls of the room; the ceiling.

'Surriya why don't you call a cab? I want to go home … '

'My love, you are very ill.' Surriya was weeping.

There were blurred faces, voices and a mist of tears. The voices were hers and Surriya's. She heard herself cry out aloud. 'Home—I want to go home—to Abba Mian.' She opened her eyes; everything was red—Surriya; the room; the ceiling. Someone helped her to stand—was she moving or had the things around her acquired feet? Houses, trees, shops, streets, everything rushed past her. Then, suddenly the movement ceased and the world stood still. A door opened. Someone supported her. She stood up. She had to cross the Ganga. They were at the ghat. She could see the wooden risers of the steps to the ferry. Step by unsteady step she walked towards them, then stopped—how could she go anywhere without her luggage—my bags; where are my bags?

A man spoke, 'I'm coming with you. Your bags are with me.'

'I don't want a porter. Give me my bags.' She grabbed the bag and pulled it away from the porter's hand.

Her hand clasped the railing and she began to climb. It was so dark—the steps swung drunkenly beneath her feet. It was a long way to her cabin—suddenly she had made it to the top—she had made it—made it—where had she made it to? Where was she going—what was her goal? She pressed the call-bell—why couldn't she move her finger away from the bell push. There was so much noise—sweat poured down her face. The river was in high flood; the ship's timbers shuddered at the impact of the rushing tide—her feet slipped on the deck—suddenly the cabin door swung open and she lost her balance. A pair of hands steadied her; she heard a woman scream. Through half shut eyes she saw Abba Mian coming towards her—she had arrived.

The pillow was damp with river-spray. She picked it up and put it on one side. The steamer was speeding down the river and the moonlit spray fanned out drenching everything. There was a tinkling of bells, Imaman bua came in holding the folds of her dress close to her. She had an iron shovel in one hand and a brass brazier in the other. She bent down to the ship's engine and began to shovel the burning embers from its furnace into the brazier. Carefully she began to spread them on the moon-silvered waves and the Ganga glowed and throbbed with rubies.

'Come!' she called. 'What are you waiting for beta? Come!'

Obediently she arose; her sari gleamed milk white in the moonlight as she placed her unshod feet on the burning coals. Across the waters Babban Mian's voice rose up in lamentation—'It is not without a cause, these echoing voids and deserted habitations—they yearn for the loved ones who quickened them with life'. She wept uncontrollably—'I sold my home Abba Mian!'

'How much did you sell it for my child?' he called out from the terrace.

'For the piece of silver and a shard of the broken clay pot pledged at my birth.'

His hands clasped behind his back Abba Mian strolled up and down the terrace. Step by step his voice descended the stairs and floated across to her, 'Too cheap. You sold it too cheap!'

The Gandhi cap on his head laughed and echoed, 'Too cheap! You sold your birthright for nothing!'

Abba Mian was angry! She must win him over—restore him to good humour. Even as she made a move towards him she awoke. It was only a dream—a mirage. The room was filled with a bluish light and the scent of lavender water. Starched white poplin blinds covered the lower half of the window. Above them she could see a sliver of sky. The night had passed. Outside the window was the tentative, uncertain light of early dawn.

Thank God, it was only a dream. Abba Mian must be at the riverside. The impress of Ganga's broad stream was upon her sleep-filled eyes. A cool breeze sprang up and caressed her body. Its waters whispered along on their course. The river must be awake.

'Freshwater fish! Fresh Fish! The voice cut across her thoughts. She heard the tinkle of a bicycle bell as the vendor called out his wares. Bemused, she listened to his cry and with a rush of memory she was back in the present, separated from the Ganga by the wilderness of exile. Abba Mian's diminishing figure receded into the distance. He had traversed an immeasurable distance. He would not return.

Abba Mian had remained constant; it was she who had turned away from all that he stood for. She had now returned to the home that welcomed her back with open arms. It was Bano Aunty and Cowas Uncle who had given her succour in her hour of need. They had brought her back to Meenu's room and to Meenu's bed.

Faces swam before her eyes and the river's cool water soothed her brow. Manuchehr, Bano Aunty, Cowas Uncle spooned food into her mouth.

The rhythmic chant of a voice raised in prayer fell upon her ears. She turned her head towards the voice. A small black cap on her head, Bano Aunty, rocked to and fro in the armchair by her bed intoning verses from the gaathas.

The cadences of her voice—the prayer—dispelled the shadows in the dimly lit room. Birjees shut her eyes, but the tears seeped from beneath the tired lids. She felt a presence close by her and looked up; Bano Aunty was bending solicitously over her. Seeing that she was awake, she kissed her forehead and drawing up her chair close to the bed sat down near her.

'How are you feeling now Birjees?' she asked, taking her hands in her own gentle, kindly ones. She was looking at her as if at a thing most dear to her. She placed a hand on her forehead, 'Praise be to Ahura Mazda, the fever has left you.' Her eyes fell on the tear-wet pillow and she stood up in agitation. 'Now you cry like a baby—and there you pretended to be grown up and travelled from country to country! You left your own land to come here, and now when you are faced with life's ups and downs, you go sniffle sniffle all over the place. Tell me, are you a grown up lady or a silly girl from some backward locality?'

Arms akimbo she glared at her before handing her the thermometer. Obediently Birjees placed it under her tongue as her eyes fell on the array of bottles and medicaments on the table.

Examining the thermometer a minute and a half later, Bano Aunty gave praise to Ahura Mazda once again, 'This is the first time your temperature has touched normal. Manuchehr has been very worried.' Shaking the thermometer briskly she replaced it in its case.

No questions were asked. Not a word said about the cause of her return, sick and distraught from the threshold where they had left her excited and happy; the home that she had called her own and where she had planned to spend her entire life. All that she talked about was their concern for her and how worried they had been—how Manuchehr had sat up nights at her bedside and how he had fetched Dr. Khambata and how relieved he had been when he had told them there was nothing for them to worry about.

Chirping away she left the room to give the good news about Birjees' fever to Cowasji and Manuchehr.

She recovered from her illness and life took on the still calm of an unruffled pond. The past was over and done with and the future stretched before like a blank page on which her life had to be written anew.

Birjees sat up as Manuchehr entered the room. He had brought her a cup of tea. The room filled with silence. Waves of claustrophobia washed over her. Head bent Manuchehr sat there silently examining his hands, then looked up and said, 'When I realised that Mr. Pervaiz was the fiancé for whom you had left India to come here, I was stunned—but there was little that I could do and nothing that I could say to you. That is why when Mummy took out your jewellery and began to pack your things, I demurred and said I would deliver your things at a later time. I knew you would come back. It is sad that the person for whom you left everything should be getting married to another girl— Mr Pervaiz' father-in-law is one of my patients—some of his medicines had to be imported for him—Pervaiz' house is closer to where I work and it was convenient for me to drop them off at his place—that is why I stopped there that day. I put Daddy in the picture as soon as I realised who Pervaiz was. He was very upset—but there was nothing we could do. Your return didn't surprise us, nor could we fail to understand the cause of your illness. All I want to say to you is, don't grieve for a man who isn't worth the cost of your tears.' He got up and left the room. The cup of tea that he had brought for himself stood there untouched.

When Surriya called, she refused to speak to her. 'Next time she calls Aunty, please tell her that I've gone away from here,' she said shuffling the pack of cards. These days she spent hours playing rummy with Mrs. Cowasji.

Qamar Bhai had also called to ask after her health, and one evening he came to see her. The nature of her illness was a mystery to him, nor could he understand why she was not at Pervaiz' house.

It was only a matter of a few weeks when Pervaiz' marriage to another girl would resolve all mysteries. Better to tell him everything herself. She found it strangely easy to talk to him.

'Unlucky man!' was his first spontaneous response. When he looked at her, there was a flicker of hope in his eyes. 'How long will you stay here now? Come home with me.'

'And how long could I stay there Qamar Bhai? Eventually I must learn to live on my own—there is little point in moving house for a few days.'

'Ours is a poor home and not what you are used to, but all your life if you …'

She did not let him complete the sentence, 'No Qamar Bhai. You are a good man and the fault does not lie with you. The trouble is with me—I would not be able to make you happy!'

Her unequivocal reply left him with nothing more to say and he took his leave. But he had been right; she could not stay here indefinitely. It was time to change her terms of reference and give a new direction to her life. But still she continued with her half-life and Cowas uncle and Bano Aunty continued to behave as if she were a permanent member of their household. Manuchehr too started coming home early from work and at his mother's insistence, drove them to the sea or took them miles away to the farmhouse of a friend. He had the harmonium repaired and tuned and she spent hours in riaz and at night Mrs. Cowasjee would ask her to sing for them.

She would get up silently and sit before the harmonium and the three would listen to her rapt. Manuchehr suggested that she audition for Radio Pakistan. He was convinced that she would be given a programme of her own. She listened to them as they discussed her music and though she did not utter a word, she knew that she had never been in better voice. Her fingers moved on the black and white keys and as she sang, a sense of deep peace entered her spirit. She had violated each rule, overstepped every established boundary and disturbed the peace of the family when she had insisted on taking singing lessons. Now that Abba Mian was no more and the family scattered to the winds, why not seek to give meaning to her life through her music.

Lying on her bed at night she would gaze at the white ceiling that had given her protection. In the sun's burning heat this roof had been her stay and shelter. But she could not stay here forever—she would have to go. The quest for life could compel one to desert the earth that held the bones of one's ancestors, but no one person merited this permanent exile. Now that Pervaiz had left her life, there was no earthly reason for remaining here. Abba Mian had gone, but the earth where he slept remained and her mother's grave lay next to his. The city of the dead had its own tenements and squares, but the living were there too—her friends, her teachers—those who had shaped her thoughts; made her what she was. They were all there!

Then why was she not with them? What was she doing here? Having arrived at a decision, she slept.

On waking she could hear Mrs. Cowasjee's voice raised in prayer in the adjoining room. The time had come when she must take leave of this voice. Tears stung her eyes at the thought. How shall I broach this topic with Cowas Uncle? What shall I say to him? Torn between silence and speech, she said nothing that day.

'It will be Manuchehr's birthday in a few days,' Mrs. Cowasjee announced over breakfast. 'We will celebrate in style and I will dress you in a gara. I have the most beautiful garas—when you see them your eyes will dazzle! Her hands busily whipping eggs for bharuchi akori, Mrs. Cowasjee chattered on. Birjees did not know what to say. She neither understood the recipe for bharuchi akori, nor did she know what a gara was. All she knew was that she was not going to talk about leaving until after the birthday celebrations were over.

Mrs. Cowasjee sliced off the top of her egg with a spoon, then stopped and glared at Manuchehr. 'I don't know anything! You want to invite your friends to Beach Luxury—done! But I want to celebrate too—and that is also done! You understand? What you want—we will do. And what I want, we will also do!' The sentence built up to a crescendo.

'But Mummy ...!'

'Are you now more of a disbeliever than your father? Has your head become the rubbish bin of all Karachi?' The bullet-fire of her attack picked up speed and Birjees began to gulp down her breakfast.

'Young Cowasjee, not another word will I listen to! If you wish to call it a dance party—or a cocktail party—do so! If you want to feed us cake and invite all the ministers—or the prime minister—do so! But I will also celebrate; and I will invite the priests, the *Raspi* and the Zaotar. It is because they do not come to this house that the blessing of Ahura Mazda has left us. They will come and perform the aachu michu ceremony.

Birjees took a large bite of the toast and got up from the table; Manuchehr's pale skin was flushed pink right down to the fine hairs on his earlobes.

'And you Birjees, where do you think you're off to? You are planning to make lemonade out of your tea—or is it to be ice cream?' She had spotted Birjees' untouched cup and turned her guns in her direction.

'I'll be back in a minute!' Excusing herself, she fled the room.

'For God's sake, Mummy! Why do you have to scold her?'

He wasn't allowed to complete his sentence—'And if *I* don't scold her, will I ask someone else to come and set her right? When your sister jumped up like that how was I expected to speak?'

'But she isn't Meenu, Mummy!'

'And who's to know that better than I? I'm tired of all your philosophy. It was all this philosophising by father and son that wrecked our family. Can't you see how her coming has brought life back to the house? When she laughs, the very walls laugh with her—when she sings the whole house fills with joy. It is as if your sister had come back to us!'

'Mummy, for God's sake!'

For sometime silence reigned supreme. Bano Lashkari Cowasjee sat there staring at the damp corner of her sari pallu with which she had wiped her eyes.

'Young Cowasjee, what do you have to say for yourself now?' she asked flicking an errant teardrop from her eye.

Clearing up in the kitchen, Birjees heard the conversation that took place between the mother and son. There was a sense of abiding permanence about the house where everything had its appointed place—it was only the people who seemed displaced—and she had appeared in their midst like a spirit or sorceress in a play erupting onto the stage from a hidden trapdoor with a tale of magical wonders and wish fulfilment. She wished she could clap her hands and say to Manuchehr, 'Go! Three miles down this path you will enter a magical world. Do not be afraid—keep walking; you will pass through a corridor of moving pictures, but don't let them distract you. Once past the corridor, you will be assailed by the sound of lamentation and weeping—not even by the flicker of an eyelid must you show that you are afraid. Only then will the magic spell be broken and the garden of delights restored to its original state. Here all wishes will be granted and losses restored and in the garden Meenu will come back to you.'

But she was no fairy-spirit or sorceress, who with a snap of her fingers could break the magic spell and restore the lost plenitude of this home. She had no power to bring back Meenu who had left them all for love of Rattan to make her own little heaven—or hell—in some unknown corner of India.

The image of a young girl grew before Birjees' eyes … delicate; graceful … 'why do you stand thus maiden?' said a voice. 'Go braid your hair—put kohl in your eyes … why wait here dreaming? The world is full of colour and music and your lover awaits you… why do you stand there with your tresses unbound?' And without a backward glance, the maiden got up and breaking all ties, left with the lover of her dreams. 'Meenu begum, is this the way to deal with loved ones?'

'When the day wanes and the sun sets and you sit in front of the harmonium and weigh your image in your Rattan Advani's eyes and the breath of a song touches your lips—is this the tale you tell? "Come one come all! Listen to my *Shahnama*—there came a merchant to the house next door; he saw me at the palace gates and was maddened with love—come one come all! It's a true story I tell—a new *Shahnama*." Surely at such moments your thoughts must sometimes look homewards.'

Faceless Time sat with the world spread beneath his feet, Tak-i-Bistan—the steps to the throne of Jamshed—iconic symbols of the Parsi world. A brightly coloured picture of this world hung in Cowasjee's study. Don't be fooled by our bowed shoulders and pale faces. We were once a powerful people—we were Khusro and Dara, of the Hall of a Thousand Pillars. Bearing rich gifts, vassals from far of climes and places came to make obeisance to the kings of kings. They toiled up the royal steps and touched their foreheads to the earth. Time, faceless Time with the world spread beneath his feet—Meenu Rattan Advani, Birjees Dawar Ali, Bano Lashkari Cowasjee—Eve and the daughters of Eve. Adam and the sons of man. Who could tell whether Meenu still knelt to the icons of this world or did she walk on the razor's edge of Pul Chinwat? Did she burn in the flames of remorse as she remembered the home that became a purgatory when she left it or did she walk in heavenly bliss?

Birjees had no answers to these questions.

It was still dark when Mrs. Cowasjee arose next day and passed the afargan of smouldering frankincense through the house before sitting down before the *Gathas*. The rise and fall of her voice mingled with the fragrant fumes: *Az tumi pursum—I ask thee Ahura Mazda*

There was so much to be done and no one to do it. The niece who had offered to help had fallen sick and all the work devolved on Mrs. Cowasjee. Birjees could assist with the preparation of the meal for the guests but was forbidden to help with the ceremonial food. 'Such a lovely girl but sadly not from among us! What a pity! She can't take part in the ritual celebrations; she can only look on –from a distance—and even that will cause raised eyebrows.'

By late afternoon most of the food had been prepared. It was now time for Mrs. Cowasjee to unlock the sideboard and take out the ceremonial silverware: bowls, ladles, tongs and afargan, the holder of the sacred fire. They hadn't been used for some time, and despite the protective cloth in which they were kept carefully wrapped, the silver had tarnished.

'Black! The climate of Bombay and Karachi is black—you can polish your silver and brass in the morning, by evening it'll have turned black!'

She had spread a sheet of cloth on the takht and the speed of her conversation matched the brisk movement of her hands polishing the silver.

'By the grace of Ahura Mazda, Manuchehr has agreed to take part in the ceremonies. It is because you're here that he has submitted so meekly—otherwise he would have raised such a hue and cry.'

Watching the rhythmic movement of her hands accompanied by the corresponding jingle of her bangles, Birjees gave voice to a request that had been in her mind for some time, 'Aunty may I go down to the shops for a bit? I'll be back in half an hour.'

'Now why would you want to do that?' The briskly moving hands stilled for a moment and a frown creased her forehead.

'I won't be long—there are a couple of books that I want to buy,' she replied, avoiding Mrs. Cowasjee's eye.

'And what if you lose your way?'

'O, come Aunty! I've been there a million times with you. How can I possibly get lost—I'm familiar with all the streets.'

'All right, baba, go. Do as you please, but go like a bullet and come back like a shot.'

Once out in the street she didn't have to wait long before she spotted an empty Victoria.

Baba take me down to Ghulam Mohammad's she instructed the ancient coachman who was squatting on his haunches.

'Yes, memsaab. Climb in.'

Placing his hands on his knees he hauled himself up and raised the hood of the buggy, then hitched himself up on to the coachman's seat. The seats of the Victoria were worn out and the discoloured upholstery was torn in places. He twitched the reins of the skeleton thin horse and the old contraption jerked into motion.

If only she had a magic wand! With one wave she would replace the buggy with her father's phaeton, its shining appointments catching the glinting sunlight, and conjure up her beloved Sitara in place of the tired old horse. Starched snow-white loose covers would replace the threadbare upholstery and in place of the old coachman, there would be Naju Chacha, now rattling his whip in its brass holder, now slicing the air with its thong, scolding, coaxing Sitara to move faster. Impossible that the thong should ever touch Sitara's side, though the noise and flurry belied such intentions. The Victoria stopped with a jerk and Sitara, Naju Chacha, phaeton and all melted away in the empty air. They had arrived at Ghulam Mohammad's.

Delhi, Patna, Lucknow, Calcutta—how many times had she not gone shopping for Abba Mian—selecting, buying cologne, collars, ties, cuff links—her eyes ranged across the various items on display and came to rest on a dressing gown of rich Chinese design with meditative old men with whispy beards and caps, willow trees in gardens, flowing streams and dragons in deep crimson, black and scarlet on a background of pale gold. It seemed a fitting gift for Manuchehr's birthday. She paid for it and stepped into the street.

Her little white lie to Bano Aunty had been necessary. Had she told her the real reason for the shopping trip, she would never have been allowed to leave the house. Her situation overwhelmed and embarrassed her. She had walked uninvited into the Cowasjees' lives, and was now acting as if she meant to spend the rest of her life with them.

On reaching home she found Bano Aunty amidst a welter of the most incredibly beautiful garas—six yards each of silk with which only rich Parsi ladies adorned their bodies and which were now becoming exceedingly rare.

'Cowasjee's father bought this for his wife in either the 1870s or '80s. He had business interests in Karachi and Bombay and travelled a lot to China and Japan. At this time Parsi folk used to buy made-to-order saris for their wives from China. Our dowries were considered incomplete without a gara,' she said, gently running reminiscent fingers across a richly embroidered black and crimson lake sari. 'Now Birjees,' she said, briskly snapping back into the present, 'choose the one you want to wear tonight. It'll depend on whether you have a matching blouse of course—this one is a chakla chakli design and this one a kanda papito garo. Which one will you wear—decide now, quickly, quickly!'

Entranced, Birjees gazed at the world of gaaj silk that populated the garas. Birds, thickets, flowering trees and plants, arched wooden bridges and pagodas, women bending in ripening fields, men with ancient beards absorbed in profound debate—glorious testimony to the skill of nineteenth century Chinese craftsmanship. But the deft fingers that had put in stitch upon careful stitch to create this populous world were stilled and clad in suits of regulation blue, Chinese women cycled to work and the men had no time to debate the precepts of Lao Zhe and Confucius. The bridge that had joined the nineteenth to the twentieth century had crumbled before the onslaught of time and history.

Come evening, and the mirror looked at Birjees and saw the richness of embroidered silk, the pallu draped on the right shoulder and the decorously covered head. She was the heroine in a production of the 'Bombay Parsi Natak Mandal' or in a play staged by the 'Parsi Alexander Theatrical Company': Birjees Lashkari Chinoy or Birjees Tanaz Minwala—who would question her identity? Life was a disguise, a mask, a mimicry—a buffoonery. Look—take note of Time's celestial capers.

Guests began to arrive and the house filled with people. Enfeebled old women, and men; pale young men and women frost bitten in their prime—the guttering lamps of a moribund race. The colossi of a world long past—the gateway of Bustan, the eternal pillars, the throne of Jamshed—they were all one with the dust. Fire worshippers—children of Zaratushtra; a dying race still snagged in history as Time's vulture pecked and pecked …

It was the first time that she saw Manuchehr in traditional Parsi clothes: long white tunic reaching well below the knees and starched white drainpipe pajamas and cap. How different he looked from the Manuchehr she saw every day at breakfast and dinner. Bano Aunty was over the moon with joy.

The religious ceremonies began. Their faces half veiled the Zaotar and Raspi sat on the corners of the square white-sheeted floor covering. The sacred fire was lit in the afargan. Round trays, one filled with fruit and flowers was placed in the centre; another containing sixteen different kinds of fruit was placed near the Raspi's left hand. In line with it lay another tray containing ritual food. He picked up pieces of sandalwood and frankincense with the silver tongs and threw them on the sacred flame in the afargan.

Fire that was Truth born of the Divine had provided the spark from which the human race had sprung. But where was the sacred fire of Behram? The sacred fire fed by sixteen different woods and resins—agarics and herbs gathered to fourteen thousand hours of continuous chanting of the Gathas. That sacred fire was lost; was a thing of the past.

Birjees observed the ceremonies from a distant corner of the drawing room—she saw the Zaotar and Raspi present flowers to each other and she looked on as they threw the sandal wood in the fire and raised their voices to intone the opening phrases of Yasna ka Baaj, the auspicious prayer, 'Humata—Hukhta—Huvarasht.'

After the ceremonies, the feasting began. Mrs. Cowasjee chirped and talked like the bird from the thousand tales of Bulbul. She took Birjees around and introduced her to the different guests. No questions were asked, but there were raised eyebrows—sometimes at her name and at others at her dress. Manuchehr was busy with his camera. He took pictures of guests and relations, of Birjees and of his parents. In one picture she posed with Mr. and Mrs. Cowasjee, in another he asked a friend to photograph him with the family and Birjees. Nusservan Pervez Cowasjee, Bano Lashkari Cowasjee, Birjees Dawar Ali, Manuchehr Nusservan Cowasjee. Smiling faces and smiling moments even as they all, birds, beasts, trees and plants, women and men were drawn inexorably down the maw of reptile time—my turn today—tomorrow it will be yours.

The sun's rays purified human habitations, gardens and ripening fields with light and the familiar smell of frankincense pervaded the house—*Az toomi pursum* ... This I ask Thee, tell me truly Ahura—this I ask Thee.

The family was at the breakfast table when she announced her decision to return to India. Cowasjee carefully folded the newspaper, removed his spectacles and focussed his attention on her.

'You will go away Birjees?' there was an ocean of disbelief in Bano Aunty's question. Her hand knocked against the tumbler splashing the table cloth. Leaving his half eaten toast on the plate, Manuchehr quietly left the room.

Suddenly wan, Bano Aunty's face was turned towards her. She couldn't understand why, when there was no one waiting for her in India, should she want to go back—why could she not remain in Pakistan?

'Cowasjee will find a job for you. Manuchehr will take you to the Radio Station; he will arrange an audition for you and you will sing on the radio. I'll look for a nice match for you through friends in the Mohammadan Society, and we'll hold a wedding reception for you in this house.

Birjees' eyes filled. Chhoti Ammi, Ashraf Chacha, Pervaiz—so many bonds, so many relationships—so many faces that had drowned in these tears. Only Bano Aunty's face survived the flood and beckoned to her. Overcome with emotion, she reached out and clasped her hand.

Visibly upset, Cowasjee got up from the table. 'Don't upset Birjees,' he admonished and left the room.

The house caught the mood from its inmates and each wall and doorway was imbued with loss. Bano Aunty retreated into silence and Cowasjee fretted about her future. Where would she go in India; with whom would she stay—what would she do?

'Give me a few days,' he said to her polishing his glasses. 'I have friends in Delhi; people I can rely on. I will see to it that some arrangements are made for your employment and accommodation.'

'I would prefer to live in Lucknow. I don't want to go back to Patna—there are too many memories there for comfort. It will be easier to start afresh in Lucknow. There are music teachers there—many of my friends live there as do many of Abba Mian's friends.' The words stuck in her throat like thorns. These were the people whom she had attempted to leave like a thief in the night in her quest for those she had thought were her own people. Nusservan Perviz Cowasjee, Muhammad Pervaiz Ashraf Ali. Connected to him with links of blood, language, religion and land, her ties with Muhammad Pervaiz were legion. Nusservan Perviz on the other hand was a stranger and unknown to her; separated from her by the distances of creed, language and country, so how were the boundaries of relationships drawn? Where did they end and where did they begin?

After dinner that night Manuchehr joined her on the balcony.

'I realise that you have been deeply hurt—but you mustn't go like this. Stay for a while; get to meet other people; interact with them—it is possible that you will find kindred souls among them.'

'Have you ever known anyone to live in a graveyard?'

'I don't understand—what do you mean?'

'My relationships, my culture, my way of life lie buried in this soil. How can I make a life among these graves?'

A silence so deep that it seemed nothing could break it fell on them. After a while, Manuchehr drew a deep breath, removed his elbows from the parapet and straightened up. 'Don't forget, no matter where you are, there is one home in this city that belongs to you.' He turned to go, and then stopped. 'The photographs of the party have been processed. I'll have one set made for you. Take them with you when you go.'

Cowas uncle looked worn out when he came home that evening. 'I have spoken to Firoze Avari. All travel arrangements have been made and you leave tomorrow. I can't take you to Delhi, but I'll accompany you to Lahore.'

'Birjees. You're going to desert this house!' Bano Aunty's voice quavered and she got up and locked herself in her room.

Impossible to explain to her the reasons for her going—impossible also to say goodbye.

'I'll write to you. In a year or so I'll come and see you.'

'You're big fraud, Birjees. You won't come. After all, what are we to you?'

The words struck her like a blow. 'What you are to me is more than all other relationships—it is something deeper and stronger than all other ties.' She was finding it hard to speak.

Manuchehr came for her luggage and silently handed her the packet of photographs. She put them in her handbag—there was no time to look at them now.

When she went to the lounge Bano Aunty made her open her suitcase and placed the priceless gara she had worn at Manuchehr's party in it. 'It is for your dowry,' she said, silencing Birjees' protests.

Manuchehr picked up her bags and left; Cowasjee had already gone down and was waiting for her by the car. Bano Aunty embraced her, kissed her forehead and placing something in her hand folded her fingers on it.

She opened her hand and saw the 'family heirloom,' the brooch that had led her to them. 'It belonged to my grandmother!' Travelling across the days and months, Cowasjee's words echoed in her ears.

'No aunty! Not this—you can't part with this! This is too much …'

'It is not a matter of too much and too little Birjees. Had Meenu left this house in the proper manner, her achoomi cho[33] would have been held and …' the rest of the sentence was lost in Bano Lashkari Cowasjee's tears. This was the first time that she had taken Meenu's name in front of Birjees and she was engulfed by a wave of pain. The turquoise brooch burnt in her hand like an ember.

Choking down her sobs, she turned a tear-drenched face towards Birjees and then pushed her out of the door. 'Now go!'

Birjees paused, turned towards her and bending down, touched her feet, and then raised her hand to her forehead before kissing the tips of her fingers. Turning she hurried down the stairs. She did not have the courage to stop for another look. In this city, the doors of this house would always open out to her like a mother's arms. Seeing her receding back, Bano Cowasjee placed a green leaf on the surface of a mirror before pouring water on it to let it float away—*mamistahim hum fardharodan nikano dilbaran o khairkhwahan ra ahu noor nigehdar badan ast mamistaham*— 'As you have turned your back on us to leave us, so may you returning, turn your face towards us.

Shoulder rubbed against shoulder at the station as the crowd milled past; the waiting train was standing on the other side of the iron grill.

Cowasjee repeated his instructions, reiterating the names of people she must meet and directions as to where she was to stay. Feroze Avari will meet you at the station. You'll have no trouble recognising him—he will be wearing a solar hat—nobody wears a solar hat and a suit any more.'

Her heart seemed to contract, she turned aside hiding her tears. Gaining control over her feelings she faced him. 'May I say something uncle?'

'But of course.'

'Let me have Meenu's address. I'd like to meet her.' She had finally worked up the courage to speak the words that she had been unable to utter in the long journey from Karachi to Lahore.

Cowasjee looked at her for a long moment. 'It won't be possible for you to meet Meenu. She committed suicide a few months after leaving home.'

Trickster-Time stood by and laughed and the sound of that laughter spread on the earth and reverberated from the skies. *Bura-ay yakkay shoran ... I Manizha, daughter of great Afrasiab who was not seen unveiled by the sun, I was dragged naked to the pit of Bizhan. He is dragged down by chains; the helpless man's clothes are soaked in his blood. Because of my anxiety for him my eyes were ever filled with tears.*

Uncomprehending, shaken to the core, Birjees looked at him. Cowasjee was wiping his spectacles with his handkerchief. 'Now go, you'll miss the train. Your aunty knows nothing. She believes Meenu is alive and happy. That knowledge is enough to sustain her life.' He gestured to the porter who balanced her suitcase on his head and started walking towards the train. As if in a trance, she moved after him. Then stopped and looked back. Cowasjee was still standing there following her with his eyes. Catching her looking at him, he quickly turned and walked away. She stood there watching his retreating back, till a wave of passengers hid him from view.

Fleetingly, the handful of days and the fistful of nights that she had passed beneath this kindly roof so many years ago, flashed before her eyes. Birjees looked at the time-ravaged figure whom she held in close embrace. These bat-like remnants of a time long past were a mockery of the remembered face. Twisted, arthritic fingers felt her body and moved up to caress her face; she felt the touch of withered lips upon her cheek as the dimmed eyes tried unsuccessfully to recognise her.

'You have come Meenu! By the grace of Ahura Mazda, you have come! But you took too long—your daddy has gone to the Tower of Silence, and I am left all alone. Your uncle has gone, Birjees, he has gone to the Tower.'

Windstorms! Earthquakes! Deserts of arid sand!

His Royal Highness Time held the megaphone as writer, producer, director and financier of the tale of life.

Come, Birjees Dawar Ali, take Meenu's skeleton out of the wardrobe; put it on, step on the stage, and play your part! Hurry! The lights are on and the camera rolling.

Life was a play and the world a stage. A performance, a mimicry a buffoonery. Look—take note of Time's celestial capers. We may put on a hundred guises, play a thousand roles—it is to no avail. Meenu, already lost in the desert sands of oblivion. Birjees, moving inexorably towards that same end. Bano Lashkari Cowasjee! Who can arrest the turning of fate? 'I, a sinner burnt in a fire ...' but what is sin and where does virtue lie? In the space that divides the good from the bad, the sacred from the profane, lies Pul Chinwat—sharper than the blade of a sword and as narrow ... and what remains is a forgetting.

Pul Chinwat. Pul Sirat. There was Meenu and there was Birjees. One was here, the other was not. She ate the flesh of fowls and there was flesh and skin on her bones. But flesh and sinew had been picked clean from Meenu's bones and her skeleton had turned to dust and ashes and lay in the ineffable depths of silence. 'I, a sinner burnt in such a fire that I became neither coal nor ashes.'

Truth and Lies. Lies and Truth. At what point did the one become the other? *Az toomi pursum—I turn to you, Ahura Mazda. Tell me. Where are lies forged? Where does truth take birth?*

A key turned in the lock. Everything was illusory—a mirage, unreal; a magical trick. Who would enter now?

The Ogre? Or the Prince? Would imprisonment be the outcome? Or freedom?

The door opened and then shut. The sound of footsteps grew louder.

Time's minion, Birjees Dawar Ali, turned and looked. Another actor had stepped onto the stage. Loosely fitted casual clothes and a stethoscope—the Christ-like mein—a second coming? The newcomer took a step forward, and then froze.

Bano Lashkari raised her head at the sound of the footsteps. 'Now come quickly! Look at her—embrace her. Your sister has come—share the grief of your father's death with her. Her voice cracked. Turning her head she called out, 'Birjees—come out of your room—my prince of Wales has come.'

Where was Bano Aunty? Where, in this ruinous body did she reside? Her eyes oceans, Birjees looked at the newcomer. .. 'A wind arose from an unknown quarter and the glory of the garden was destroyed'. His lips moved. Her fingers flew to her lips. Careful! Careful! Don't say a word.

'Meenu! Meenu!' Bano Aunty was speaking to her. What could she say—all that remained was a forgetting. She removed her fingers from her lips. To whom did these fingers belong—to her—or to Meenu? Were they attached to her hand or did they belong to the depths of the Tower of Silence?

'I can't believe my eyes!' he came and stood by her.

'So, you recognised me?'

'I, Manuchehr Nusservan Cowasjee' am the one who waits. How would I not recognise you?'

Birjees Dawar Ali-Alone looked at the man of whom she had taken leave half a lifetime ago … and who had said to her, 'don't go yet—wait a while; meet new people, deal with them—it is possible that here too you will find congenial souls.' … who had sent her news of his father's death and whose greeting card and found her at the beginning of each new year—perhaps only to remind her that even in this unkind city, there was a home she could call her own.

Skeleton fingers grasped his hand, 'your father said Meenu had forgotten us—would never come to see us. Now go to the Tower of Silence and tell him, mummy's won. All his life your attorney general father lied to me. All his life! Now I'll take Meenu to him and show him her face.'

Weaving its web of the passing minutes, days, centuries, eons, Spider-Time cast a glance at them—at Bano Lashkari, at Birjees at Manuchehr, each one shrouded in ignorance—each one unknowing—unaware, caught in the web of illusion like the unending row of countless others.

Life—events repeated themselves—the father had retrieved her luggage from PIB Colony, the son from the Marriott.

Seated in the rocking chair, her fingers twined in Birjees' fingers, Bano Aunty talked away—sometimes to Meenu— at other times to Birjees. An endless stream of words poured from the dry lips; but what remained was a forgetting.

Manuchehr brought her supper in a tray, but she refused to leave the rocking chair, and when Birjees held her by the arm and tried to help her up she pushed away her hand and scolded, 'Shame on you Meenu, are you now going to start bullying your old mummy?'

Disconcerted, she dropped her arm and stepped back. Manuchehr gestured to her to remain silent, then tied a napkin under his mother's chin and fed her spoonful by slow spoonful. The fastidious Bano Aunty of bygone days had dropped out of life into the crevasses of time. In her place was an old woman whose wits were addled by sorrow and who had only a few tatters of memory to call her own.

After a few reluctant morsels, she pushed the food away. Manuchehr removed the tray and coaxed her into swallowing her medicine—pills to smooth out the ravelled skein of pain—bearing the promise of sleep.

Birjees remained by her side responding to questions born of unawareness with deliberate answers based on understanding.

'How many children do you have?'

'Three!'

'Why didn't you bring them with you?'

'They're coming next week mummy.'

'And how is Rattan?'

'Well.'

'Where is your house located in Bombay?'

'Malabar Hills.'

Where was truth? Where does it reside? The world we know is a snare; a trick of the mind ... what remains in the end is a forgetting.

Bano Aunty sat and rocked in the rocking chair and talked of times past and people long gone.

Manuchehr peeped in and gestured to her come out.

'I'll be back in a minute,' she comforted and made to rise.

Fingers tightened their hold on her hand, 'You'll go now and never come back.'

'I'm not going anywhere mummy, Manuchehr is calling me—I'll be back in a minute.'

'All right, go. Ahura Mazda be praised that you have come. I had forgotten, go and send Birjees to me.'

'Yes mummy.' Wiping away her tears she left the room.

The table had been formally laid with silver and napery.

'Such a grand spread! What was the need?'

'Grand spread is it? Everything's out of the deep freezer and through the microwave. There would have been a spread indeed, if only you'd told us you were coming.'

She recalled the warmth and good cheer of mealtimes at this table. Carcases of bygone mornings and evenings went past her eyes. Like two battered survivors of life they sat down to fulfil the ritual of eating.

'When you left, you said "how can I make a life among graves." I have never forgotten your remark.'

'I remember—but Manuchehr, now everything that we lived by is dead. Centuries ago, when Alexander's armies devastated Persia, the fire that razed the hall of a thousand pillars was so powerful that it entered the very foundations of those pillars, but we have needed no external force to destroy our way of life. The buildings have remained—it is the culture that has been lost. It was our own people who set our house on fire.' Manuchehr's questions were unending—you are sifting ashes my friend, there is neither passion here nor desire. 'You are piling question upon question, tell me about yourself instead.'

'What is there to tell—I am the one who waits—there is nothing left to say.'

'Why do you call yourself the one who waits? Bano Aunty is the one who has waited all these years, and today when her waiting has ended, it is by a fraud—a mirage.'

'For you it may be a fraud—a mirage—but it is her truth and that is enough for her—today a life time of yearning has ended for her and all losses have been met.'

He smiled sadly, 'you were so wrapped up in your own loneliness that you had no time for another's loss. When did you ever think of anyone else?' He got up, 'I'm going to put mummy to bed. She usually nods off in the rocking chair. If she happens to awake when I move her, she scolds me for thinking her a cripple.'

Birjees put the leftovers in the fridge and took the used plates to the kitchen but put off the washing up for later. She wanted to take a look at Bano Aunty in case she was awake.

Manuchehr was standing by her chair looking at her.

'You still haven't moved her to her bed?'

'Mummy's sleeping,' he replied.

'Then speak softly; you'll awaken her.'

'She's gone to sleep forever Birjees.' His voice was tremulous.

Shaken, Birjees looked at the sleeping one. Her eyes were shut, the head a little to the side. Death had smoothed out the fretful lines from her face and made it soft and peaceful.

They stood beside her, arid-eyed like the June sky even as the heart's monsoon gave them a lie. Taking him by the arm she led him into the lounge. There they sat side by side with silence as the chief mourner. How imperceptibly, silent-footed life had tip toed out of this house.

Suddenly Manuchehr shook himself and stood up, 'can you stay here by yourself, or will you come with me?'

'How can I leave her by herself? You go.'

'I don't even know what to do, what the ritual observances are. Mummy's cousin lives in Defence—I'll go and fetch her, and I'll inform uncle Ardeshir. They'll see to the arrangements.'

'Tell me where the frankincense is kept. I'll see to that."

He took out the afargan and frankincense from the kitchen cupboard and handed them to her. 'She aired the house with frankincense this morning. She would drag herself around the house attending to the chores. People hang on to life because they love it—she clung to life awaiting Meenu's return. She wasn't sure whether he was talking to himself or to her.

Birjees lit the frankincense and placed the smoking censer to Banu Aunty's room, then sat down near her feet and waited. Mingling with the smoke the kindly voice echoed in her ears, 'Birjees …'

Bano Aunty was sitting by her pillow, rocking to and fro, intoning prayers for her health … now she was placing the priceless hundred year old sari in her suitcase, 'it is for your dowry' … she was tucking the her grandmother's brooch in her hand and praying for her safe journey.

Birjees touched the brooch that had brought her to them, and clasped the rigid hand in her own. 'What shall I do—what prayer shall I say for you? To which god should I make my appeal?'

She thought of the books in Cowas uncle's library—the many Persian texts that lay side by side with legal tomes. She knew she would find the Gathas among them. Perhaps these books were still there—she got up to fetch the Gathas.

She pressed the switch and the room sprang to life. The law books had given way to books on medicine, but the Farsi books were still there. Zarathushtra's portrait was still there; her eyes turned to the remaining walls and surprise held her still. They were covered with black and white photographs. Somewhat dimmed by time and a faint covering of dust, but easily recognisable. She saw herself standing there with her arms around Bano Aunty and Cowas Uncle—all three were smiling, here she was again, this time with the three of them. She saw herself in the gara, its pallu draped decorously on her head ... Birjees Tanas Minwala ... then another large portrait of herself and Manuchehr ... one by one, the veils dropped from her eyes.

Birjees, who thought of herself as alone, felt the ground slide beneath her feet and the sky bend over her. .. *Khabar i tahaiyarae ishq sun—Na janoon raha na pari rahi—Na to tu raha na to main raha—Jo rahi so bekhabri rahee. Wo ajab ghari thi ke jis ghari—Liya dars nuskha i ishq ka—Ke kitab aqal ki tak par—joon dhari the toon he dhari rahi— observe, the amazing transformations of love, All passion spent—the dream fled. We moved beyond the 'you' and 'I'– what remained was an unknowing. Strange the moment—the moment love's lesson was learnt—unheeded on the shelf lay the Book of Reason.*

She leant against the wall for support as the empty years mocked and mimicked her like a horde of monkeys. Manuchehr gazed at her ... and I will be one with the dust by the time the news reaches you.

It was Bano Aunty who was one with the dust, who had kept faith all these years sustained by the heart's truth and who slept peacefully now that the waiting was over. With bedimmed eyes she looked for the *Gathas*, drew the book out of the shelf and turned to go, then stopped for one last look at Manuchehr, the one who waited. Oblivion was far better than this knowledge, this unquiet awareness.

She sat at Bano Aunty's feet, the open *Gathas* in her lap, softly her voice picked up the cadences of the prayer, '*behtreen cheez naseeb o baad aara ke arzoo-i- bahisht ast ...*

*and it shall be for him the best of all things. After his longing
for bliss may one be given bliss, through the most provident
most holy spirit...* (Avesta: Yasna: 43:2)

Bano Aunty was stroking her head. 'You have come
Birjees; you have brought Meenu with you...'

Before her eyes, the mound of earth that was Abba Mian;
beside it another mound which was the woman who had
given birth to her—whose love she had never known—the
same woman was leaving her once again—that time she
had been laid in the earth, now she would be placed on an
iron frame. The worms had devoured her then, now the
birds of the air would feed on her. The *Gathas* slipped from
her nerveless hands.

The sun had lost its heat by the time a tired Manuchehr
looked upon his mother; the ceremonial pall bearers were
taking her to the Tower of Silence—Burj-e-Khamoshi,
Dakhma—three names for the same destination. Thirty
steps behind his mother were the two priests intoning
the funerary prayer. He followed as part of the funeral
procession repeating the prayer along with others of the
community. Knowing that she could not take part in any
ritual, Birjees had looked her last on Bano Aunty earlier.

He watched as his mother was placed on a stone slab;
the last rites were performed and her face was covered. He
would never see her again. The door of the Tower opened
and she was carried inside. The priests would now place
her on the iron shafts of the grill. After a lifetime of longing
this would be her resting place. He looked up and saw the
clear blue sky—high up above him a few vultures circled

in the air. There were others lower down; some on the trees and others on the parapets of the Tower. Symbols of mortality—of life's transience—the vultures gazed upon their impending meal with unambiguous singleness of purpose. He had heard it said it was the eyes they picked at first. A shudder ran through his frame. Time had stolen a march on Death; robbed of their dreams the vacant orbs were all that was left for the vultures' feast.

At home, Meher aunty and uncle Ardeshir were in charge of the post funerary rituals crowding out all thought, leaving neither time nor space to grieve for his mother or rejoice in Birjees' presence. Why was it that sorrow and joy always came hand in hand? Two days fled by as if they had never been.

The eve of departure—the airport—when Birjees had left them for the first time, he had wanted to accompany her to Lahore instead of his father, but had been unable to broach the matter with him. Perhaps if they had travelled together—alone—without the watchful presence of others, he would have had the chance to reveal his feelings to her. And now, when both time and circumstance conspired to provide him with the opportunity to speak of what was in his heart—the time to do so had gone by.

So many dreams and desires—if only she had stayed.

'What made you come back now—after so long an absence?'

'For me, this home stood for the truth of the heart's ᵗections. Setting aside the bonds of blood and nurturance; ᵗedges made at birth, the prohibitions of religion, and divisions of language and culture—they took a lost and homeless girl to their hearts—and asked nothing in return. I came as a pilgrim to this threshold—to pay homage to all that I received.'

Birjees bowed her head. The unsaid arose before her eyes like a wall. An untold tale—it had taken a lifetime to be heard. She looked at Manuchehr—if only you had spoken …

Her luggage had been checked in and passengers were making their way to the waiting plane—yet they remained, oblivious to the hustle and bustle of departure, held together by disjointed phrases—inconsequential, irrelevant. The final boarding call broke into their space; shaken, forsaken by words, they stared at each other—was this then all there was to life? A handful of days and a fistful of nights of unspoken desires awaiting recognition.

Two solitary souls looked at each other and succumbed to Time's beat. Birjees began to walk towards the silvered tube of the plane's interior—before stepping into its fiery maw, she turned and looked at the mirrored hall for her last view of Bano Lashkari's city with misted eyes. She envied her death's merciful oblivion.

Seen through an ocean of tears, Manuchehr's face wavered and became unsteady; she saw him raise his hand in a farewell gesture before he was hidden by a wave of laughing travellers. She turned and resumed her walk towards the waiting plane. Solitary, each inexorable step taking her further down Time's rapacious maw.